Do You Love Your
M🧡M
and Her Two-Hit
Multi-Target
Attacks
?

Dachima Inaka

Illustration by **Iida Pochi.**

"I merely want to tease you, Masato…"

SHIRASE

Mother of a five-year-old girl. Never passes up an opportunity to tease Masato.

"It's time you fooled around with a friend's mom."

KAZUNO

Wise's mother. Her years of experience in host clubs mean she's in her element.

DEATHMOTHER

Porta's mother wants to pay Masato back for all he's done for her daughter—and that has made this mother bold.

"These are for you, on the house."

"You *gotta* listen, or else I'm gonna bite your ear off!"

MEDHIMAMA

Medhi's mother. Can't hold her liquor. Usually very strict, but gets super clingy when tipsy.

"M-Mommy...
i-isn't sure. I'll...
have to sleep
on it..."

MAMAKO OOSUKI

The hero's mother.
Adventuring with him in the
game world has made him
grow up—and part of her is
struggling with the resulting
sadness.

"I got to
thinking
maybe it's
time I started
planning for
what comes
next."

MASATO OOSUKI

Son of the world's strongest
mother. His father has become
the Demon Lord, and in the
middle of their final quest,
Masato has started thinking
about the future.

'Twas the Edo period. A mother and child strode through the gardens of Edo Castle, bedecked with cherry blossoms.

The mother was Lady Mamako, spouse of the seventh Edo shogun.

Her child: the eighth shogun, Masato Oosuki.

A shogunal family.

"Hark, the petals dance. How lovely! …Oh my, Ma-kun. Let me clean your ears."

"I fail to see the connection between flower viewing and ear excavations."

The attending retainers moved swiftly, placing mats in the garden and preparing the ear-picking apparatus.

Masato placed his head upon Lady Mamako's lap. The gentle scraping proved quite comforting.

'Twas a quiet afternoon in each other's company.

"Peace in Edo is a blessing, granting us this relaxing moment together."

"Perhaps too relaxing. I grow drowsy…"

Masato yawned and stretched. Then…

"Cease your yawning!"

"The castle town is in an uproar, but the lords care not."

"Lord Masato! An incident is upon us!"

Wise, Medhi, and Porta—three young ninjas—appeared atop the roof. They leapt down, landing on Masato.

"Gah! …Hey, mind your landings!"

"Eep! S-sorry!"

"You I don't mind, Ninja Porta. It's the other two…"

"Yeah, yeah, sorry, sorry. But the trouble's real."

"Lady Mamako, our report. Someone has been attacking citizens in Edo town—and reports claim the perpetrator is a hideous monster."

"My word! How awful."

"Ho, Ninja Medhi. Why do you report this to my mother? I am right here. I'm the shogun—this is my purview!" Masato rose to his feet, indignant. "Ninja Porta! Fetch my weapon!"

"Yes, sir! Right away!"

Ninja Porta reached into the mysterious cloth satchel at her hip and pulled out the Holy Katana, Fuirumamento.

Blade in hand, Masato rushed through the gates and into the town below. There, he found a furry abomination, half wolf, half bear—and all ferocity.

"Halt, foul creature! I am shogun here, and I shall be your foe. Prepare thyself!"

Firm hand on hilt, he attacked, swinging unfettered…!

Then a great number of rock spikes thrust upward beneath the fiend's feet, and the skies filled with orbs of water. The creature was instantly dispatched at the hands of none other than—

"Ma-kun, you're so reckless. You know you can always leave the dangerous work to Mother."

In one hand, she grasped a fiery crimson cherry tree branch; in the other, a branch of the deepest blue. There stood Lady Mamako, wielding the two Holy Branches. She smiled, her footsteps ever so graceful.

"Come, Ma-kun. Let us return to the castle and finish cleaning your ears."

"Argh… I was in the mood for a skirmish, too… Alas, I've been fettered again!"

But Lady Mamako linked her arm firmly in his, and they headed home, surrounded by cheering crowds.

The people called Lady Mamako…the Unfettered Shogun's Mother.

Do You
Love the
Unfettered
Shogun's
Mom?

CONTENTS

Dachima Inaka

VOLUME 11

DACHIMA INAKA

Illustration by IIDA POCHI.

YEN ON

New York

Do You Love Your Mom and Her Two-Hit Multi-Target Attacks?, Vol. 11

▶ Dachima Inaka

▶ Translation by Andrew Cunningham

▶ Cover art by Iida Pochi.

TSUJO KOGEKI GA ZENTAI KOGEKI DE 2KAI KOGEKI NO OKASAN WA SUKI DESUKA? Vol. 11
©Dachima Inaka, Iida Pochi. 2020
First published in Japan in 2020 by KADOKAWA CORPORATION, Tokyo.
English translation rights arranged with KADOKAWA CORPORATION, Tokyo,
through TUTTLE-MORI AGENCY, INC., Tokyo.

English translation © 2021 by Yen Press, LLC

First Yen On Edition: November 2021

Yen On is an imprint of Yen Press, LLC.
The Yen On name and logo are trademarks of Yen Press, LLC.

The publisher is not responsible for websites (or their content) that are not owned by the publisher.

Library of Congress Cataloging-in-Publication Data
Names: Inaka, Dachima, author. | Pochi., Iida, illustrator. | Cunningham, Andrew, 1979– translator.
Title: Do you love your mom and her two-hit multi-target attacks? / Dachima Inaka ; illustration by Iida Pochi. ; translation by Andrew Cunningham.
Other titles: Tsujo kogeki ga zentai kogeki de 2kai kogeki no okasan wa suki desuka?. English
Description: First Yen On edition. | New York : Yen On, 2018–
Identifiers: LCCN 2018030739 | ISBN 9781975328009 (v. 1 : pbk.) | ISBN 9781975328375 (v. 2 : pbk.) | ISBN 9781975328399 (v. 3 : pbk.) | ISBN 9781975328412 (v. 4 : pbk.) | ISBN 9781975359423 (v. 5 : pbk.) | ISBN 9781975359430 (v. 6 : pbk.) | ISBN 9781975306311 (v. 7 : pbk.) | ISBN 9781975306328 (v. 8 : pbk.) | ISBN 9781975318413 (v. 9 : pbk.) | ISBN 9781975318437 (v. 10 : pbk.) | ISBN 9781975318451 (v. 11 : pbk.)
Subjects: LCSH: Virtual reality—Fiction.
Classification: LCC PL871.5.N35 T7813 2018 | DDC 895.63/6—dc23
LC record available at https://lccn.loc.gov/2018030739

ISBNs: 978-1-9753-1845-1 (paperback)
        978-1-9753-1846-8 (ebook)

10 9 8 7 6 5 4 3 2 1

LSC-C

Printed in the United States of America

▶ Yen On
150 West 30th Street, 19th Floor
New York, NY 10001

▶ Visit us at yenpress.com
facebook.com/yenpress
twitter.com/yenpress
yenpress.tumblr.com
instagram.com/yenpress

Prologue   A Certain Boy's Answers

Are you close to your mother?
Well, we're not *distant.*
Do you talk with your mother? How often?
We talk surprisingly normally.
Has your mother said anything lately that made you happy?
She said I'd grown up. Made me kinda happy that she noticed.
Has your mother said anything lately that made you unhappy?
She's still calling me by that nickname, but...I guess I don't mind.
Do you ever go shopping with your mother?
I carry her stuff a lot (but no more peak-hour grocery store runs, please).
Do you help your mother?
I dunno if it's actually much help, but I try.
What does your mother like?
Housework and bargain sales...and spending time with her son.
What does your mother hate?
Roaches in the kitchen.
What are your mother's strong points?
There's a lot. Can't list them all here because there's not enough space.
What are your mother's weak points?
She's got a few, but I can deal.

If you went on an adventure with your mom, would you become closer?

Chapter 1   Maybe a Real Hero Is Someone Brave Enough to Include "Hero" in Their Work History.

On the northernmost cape of the continent, a ford appears for a few scant minutes each day, giving access to lands farther north.

Here lie sheer cliffs, marking the farthest corners of the world. Stairs built in days of yore stretch to the clouds above.

The stairs themselves are decorated with constellations and depictions of celestial bodies. What awaits at the summit?

Well, the Hero, Masato, was climbing them to find out.

"We've come pretty far, but still can't see the top... Everyone doing all right?"

He glanced back and realized his party were lagging behind.

The Sage, Wise, and the Cleric, Medhi, both looked pretty tired.

"Gawd, Masato!" Wise complained. "Would it kill you to go a little slower?"

"The dungeon isn't going anywhere," Medhi chided him. "There's no need to rush."

"Yeah, I know, but... Look, I just wanna get there already! We haven't done a real quest in ages! Like, a normal one with no rebellions or family problems involved. Aren't you guys pumped?!"

"Sure, part of me feels that way...," Medhi replied.

"And if that's not enough, this leads to Heaven's Ruins! C'mon, doesn't that sound exciting?! Rahhhhhh! Heaven's Ruins! I'm coming for you!"

"That's *just* you," said Wise.

"No, come on, you gotta be—"

"Masato," Medhi interrupted, "that's *only* you. Quit focusing on your own fun and look behind us."

He did, and saw the Traveling Merchant, Porta, and Mamako, holding her hand.

Porta seemed to have plenty of energy left, but Mamako was looking worn out.

"This is what happens when you sacrifice sleep in order to fulfill your beloved son's selfish little wishes," said Wise.

"She had to make lunches, do the laundry, clean—even Mamako has her limits," Medhi added. "No matter how self-indulgent her son's requests are."

"Gah..."

This hit too close to home.

But Masato only waffled for a second. Then he turned around and ran back down to Porta and Mamako.

"Oh, Masato! Why'd you run back down here?"

"It just kinda felt right. Mom, you okay?"

"Oh my! Are you worried about Mommy? How nice! You're such a good boy!" Mamako was moved to blubbering tears.

"Spare me the waterworks. Here." Masato turned his back to Mamako and knelt down.

"Oh my! What's this?"

"You seem tired, so I'm gonna carry you. What else does it look like?"

"Ma-kun...!"

"Not that I have to or anythiiiiing!"

It started with rather large boobs laying themselves out there, one on each shoulder. Then Mamako's arms took a firm grip on his back.

"I can't believe you're doing this for me, Ma-kun! I must be dreaming! *Sniff!*" More tears.

"Please, you don't need to get worked up every time. This is totally normal! Okay, standing up now!"

"Go right ahead."

Masato flexed his legs and got to his feet. It was easier than he'd expected.

Mom's...awfully light.

Most of Mamako's weight was in her boobs, but the total package was pretty light. Definitely not a challenge for him to carry piggyback.

"Thank you kindly, young Ma-kun."

"What's with the old lady voice?!"

"Hee-hee. Just joshing with you! But these old bones can rest now."

"You're way ahead of yourself. You're in your prime!"

"And it'll be gone before you know it."

"You're one gloomy grandma!"

He could see Mamako's face out of the corner of his eye. "I bet you'll look exactly the same no matter how old you get," he said.

"I wouldn't be so sure." But it seemed terrifyingly probable.

Then she began rubbing his head. "You know, before we started this game, I never would have dreamed you would carry me like this one day."

"Yeah…I wouldn't have seen this happening, either."

"We've traveled together, met so many other families, solved so many problems…"

"And in the process, we sorted out our own issues."

Mother and child stared up at the path ahead together.

From the cliff face they could see sky, clouds, sea, and land—the world inside this game.

By their side, Porta was smiling happily. A few steps ahead, Wise and Medhi were nodding approvingly.

A world of adventure. Bonds between party members. Bonds between parent and child.

Masato had gained so much here.

The government had carried out an anonymous survey that he'd accidentally written his name on—which was but one cause.

But Mom also applied on her own.

A sudden wave of gratitude hit him, and he went to voice that thought—

—when a horrible screech shook the air. It sounded like the death throes of some wild beast.

"Oh, monsters incoming! Careful!" Porta's eyes had swiftly located the source. She was pointing at the sky above the staircase.

A massive roc was diving right at them, its wingspan clearly over ten yards wide. Totally a boss-class foe.

Combat began; Porta quickly evacuated. Wise pulled out her magic tome, Medhi her staff, and all braced for impact.

Masato wasn't about to be outdone. He was the Hero of the Heavens!

"Come at me, flying enemies! You're all mine! …Mom!"

"Got it! Time for my attack! Hyah!"

"No, I meant if you could just get off my back—!"

But before he could finish, Mamako sprang into action.

She swung Terra di Madre, the Holy Sword of the Earth—and tons of rock spikes shot out the cliff face, skewering the entire bird. The massive boss crumbled, turning into a pile of gems.

The party defeated the boss that was guarding the entrance to Heaven's Ruins!

"Hee-hee-hee! Ma-kun, Mommy did it!"

"Y-yeah, just like always… *This* never changes…"

Masato and Mamako were now a happy family. Masato had matured immensely. He no longer threw a fit about these little things. He took them in stride. Not at all frustrated.

But his gratitude from earlier? He left that unsaid.

The party resumed their climb.

They were now high enough to touch the clouds, but still the stairs went on.

Wise and Medhi had been tired to begin with. Porta had been enjoying the climb, but even she was starting to look worn out. The whole vibe was getting increasingly sluggish.

But up ahead…

"Mom, what do you think we'll find in Heaven's Ruins? I can't wait!"

"Mommy is having so much fun watching you have fun! Hee-hee!"

"With a name like Heaven's Ruins, this place has gotta be made for me! I know it!"

"True! You're the Hero chosen by the Heavens, Ma-kun! Hee-hee."

"That I am! I'm the Hero of the Heavens! Legends say these ruins have something that'll make the Hero of the Heavens cry with joy… Isn't that exciting?!"

"I'm sure you'll be ever so delighted. I can't wait to see that! Hee-hee."

Masato still had Mamako on his back, and they were chugging along, chattering away. He thought he heard two dramatic sighs from pretty far behind him, but he chalked it up to his imagination and paid it no mind.

He kept the pace up until they broke through the clouds.

And before them stood a large stone door, emblazoned with a sun and a moon—rather like Firmamento, the Holy Sword of the Heavens.

"Wow! There's gotta be *something* here! …Mom!"

"You're right!"

Masato had been less after her agreement than nudging her to get down off his back, but she didn't move from her perch. He decided that wasn't a big deal, and kept carrying her up to the door.

It was firmly closed.

"How do we open it? …Oh, right! The request said something."

He pulled out the request papers and read them over.

This was an investigation quest, and the notes explained how to get to their destination—and a requirement. To clear the dungeon, the party must have at least one Hero.

Just to be sure, he passed Mamako the paper and had her check it over. "That's what it says?" "That's what it says." The only requirement was a Hero's presence.

"We've met the conditions…so do I have to prove I'm a Hero or something?"

Worth a shot.

Firmamento served as proof that Masato was Hero of the Heavens, so he drew the blade and held it aloft.

And then he addressed the door. "My name is Masato. As you can see, I'm the Hero chosen by the Heavens."

"He's the Hero, and I'm the Hero's Mommy. Isn't my son the greatest? Hee-hee-hee."

"Mom, best if you stay out of this one. This is important. Once again… Heaven's Ruins! Heed my call, and open the way!"

And the stone door…

Did absolutely nothing.

"H-huh. That's weird…I thought for sure that would do it."

Maybe it would open at the Hero's touch.

He touched it. Didn't work.

Maybe you had to touch the Holy Sword to the door.

He did just that. Didn't work.

He tried knocking. Didn't work. Tried brute force. To no avail. Tried pulling really hard. No good. Even yelled, "Open sesame!" Stayed closed.

He tried begging with tears in his eyes. "Please, door, open!"

It remained unmoved.

"Wh-whyyyyyyyy?! I'm the Hero of the Heaveeeeeens! That's my whole thiiiing!"

"Ma-kun, don't worry. Just settle down. Even if you're not the Hero of the Heavens, Mommy's still proud of you."

"You're making it wooooooorse!"

"Geez, Masato. You're so loud. What are you screeching about now?" The girls had finally caught up.

Masato no longer had the capacity for explaining things. Mamako had to do it for him. She handed Wise the quest papers.

The three girls all put their heads together and pored over them.

"Normal quest stuff. Not one of Shiraaase's traps."

"We wanted to do a normal quest for once, so we specifically picked this one out at the Catharn Adventurers Guild as we normally do. There shouldn't be anything strange about it…"

"Oh! Wait!" Porta's sharp eyes spotted something at the bottom of the page.

There was a warning handwritten in tiny letters in the very narrow margin:

※Quest not always available. For details, speak to the mysterious nun at the nearest guild.

There you had it.

"Hmmm," Wise mused. "The penmanship's kinda familiar…"

"Porta, can you appraise this note and see who wrote it?" Medhi asked.

"Yes… That's Ms. Shiraaase's handwriting…"

Sobbing, Masato slapped the ground—earning himself some looks of genuine pity.

The party used transport magic to warp back to the nearest town.

Masato was in full-on rampage mode, and no one was even trying to stop him. He charged right through the doors of the guild…!

And found a mysterious nun calmly enjoying hot beverages in the dining area. Shiraaase gave him a wave that screamed "yoo-hoo."

"Shiraaase! What is your damn problem?!"

"Whatever do you mean?"

"Drop the act! This crap! Right here!" He slammed the quest papers down before her placid face!

"Ah yes, a quest," she said, unmoved.

"It sure is! But that ain't the problem—the problem is what you wrote here! We got to Heaven's Ruins and the door wouldn't open! Even though I, the Hero, was in the party!"

"And when we checked the quest papers over..."

"There was a note clearly in your handwriting."

"I'd know your writing anywhere!"

"So we thought we'd come pick your brain, Ms. Shiraaase! If you've got any infooormation, Ma-kun would really like to hear it."

"Aha. That would explain it." Shiraaase nodded, as if she'd just now connected the dots.

And then she leaned way back in her chair, peering down her nose at them.

"Taking your frustrations out on me is entirely inappropriate. I deserve nothing less than your gratitude! This quest is completely, thoroughly legitimate! I have not tampered with the contents at all! I merely added a supplemental note out of the goodness of my heart!"

"Er...d-did you, now?" Masato asked.

"Indeed I did. Certainly, only Masato can accept this quest, and I *was* hoping that allowing you to make that futile climb would buy me time to make preparations on my end..."

"Sorry, did you say something?"

"Never mind. I said nothing about my hidden desires manifesting themselves in the form of very small writing. Long story short, this *is* a real quest, and I have hidden no traps within. That much is true."

"Okaaay...then I'll believe *that* part." Masato was still very suspicious about the rest.

Shiraaase shot him the most beautiful smile she had ever displayed.

"Then let me infooorm you what a little bird told me."

"Tch, don't think an ultra-rare smile will get you off the hook! I refuse to give in—!"

"Why would the path not open despite the Hero's presence? I know the answer."

"Okay, I give. I do want to know that. Lay it on us."

"The reason is simple. Masato, open your stat menu."

"My stat menu?"

Masato flicked a finger in the air in front of him, pulling up the holographic menu.

The screen showed his HP, MP, STR, DEF, equipment—all information and statistics about his character.

But his job name was missing.

"The heck? Is this a bug?"

"To be blunt, yes. Thanks to your help, the game is currently in the final stages of beta testing, headed for the official release. We're currently undergoing a full-scale system check. Many game features are being reviewed and rebooted. But this has caused a few side effects—"

"So basically Masato—and only Masato—had his job reset? That's *rich*! *Snort*. Sucks to suck!"

"No, the same issue affects everyone in this world."

"What?" Wise's grin faded as she opened her own menu. "Oh crap, it's true!" She, too, had no job.

Porta and Medhi followed suit, looking flustered.

"Eep! I'm unemployed!"

"I know it's just a game job, but this is quite unpleasant..."

"It is merely a display issue, and the skills and equipment limitations the jobs provide remain functional. Don't take it *too* hard," said Shiraaase. "Mamako, how does yours look?"

"Let's see..."

Mamako opened her menu. Where it once had said "Normal Hero's Mother," it now read:

Ma-kun's Mommy

That was new.

Even Shiraaase winced a bit. "I heard the lead griping that something was preventing them from reinstituting all the jobs, but...it appears this is the cause. Mamako set a new job all on her own."

"Mom, why? How is that even possible? Fess up!"

"Mommy didn't do a thing! But Mommy *is* Ma-kun's mommy, so nothing here seems wrong to me!" She smiled blissfully.

"Not an answer."

"No matter the time or the place, even if it is merely a field on her menu, Mamako's role remains unwavering," Shiraaase explained. "That is her power as a mother: the power to make the impossible possible. No different from what came before."

"Yeah, it's just Mamako being Mamako."

"She's a stable presence."

"Yes! That describes Mama perfectly!"

Everyone gathered around Mamako, smiling. A happy ending! "No, seriously, this isn't funny," Masato interjected, but...she was his mother, and he couldn't stop himself from smiling. They lived happily ever after.

Then Shiraaase clapped her hands, forcing the attention back on her. "Now that you're aware of the problem, I can infooorm you of the solution. As the admins are unable to apply an easy fix, I'm afraid you'll all be required to manually reregister."

"And how do we do that?" Masato asked.

"You will have to participate in the job fair being held in the Catharn capital convention center."

"The what?" said Wise. "You mean, we've gotta go job hunting?"

"Fear not. The procedure is simple. You need merely to find the window for your occupation and put in an application. However, by way of apology, we are offering a one-time-only chance to change your game job, so the representatives will be making pitches as well."

"Then that makes it sound safe enough," said Medhi.

"What a relief!" Porta agreed.

"Glad to hear it. Just...one thing to be wary of."

"Oh? What's that?" Mamako asked.

Shiraaase summoned that top-notch smile again. Masato was instantly concerned. No, not concerned—terrified.

As everyone held their collective breath, Shiraaase's smile took on a diabolical edge.

"Each job can only be held by a limited number of people. If you don't register quickly, others might snatch your occupations from you! On your marks—go!"

"Arghh, Shiraaase! We'll get you for this later!"

The party turned and raced out of the guild.

A quick transport spell, and they were outside the capital.

They would have loved nothing more than to make a beeline for the convention center, but…

"Yikes, what's all this?!"

The crowds were *insane*.

Adventurers, villagers, city folk. The streets packed with people, papers in hand. There was no way through.

"I get the adventurers, but…all the ordinary NPCs, too?"

"Ms. Shiraaase did say this bug affects everyone…," Medhi pointed out. "If the system also treats 'villager' as a job, then they might need to reregister as well."

"So everyone in the entire world is here? Yeah, no wonder the place is packed," said Wise.

"Oh! I recognize some of them!" Porta was pointing at a group of villagers—including one old man leaning on a staff.

"My, if it isn't the Maman Village elder! Hello there!"

"Hrm? …Ah, Mamako! And the children. It's simply been ages!"

"Even village elders have to reregister?"

"Indeed we do. But in my case…"

With an embarrassed smile, he held up his paperwork. It had a résumé—and an application for a transfer.

And in the field for his new job title, it said: Mayor.

"I heard the tales of your exploits and decided there was more that I could do! Even at my age, one should not lose ambition! Oh, listen to me, making speeches already."

"That's perfectly all right. And a lovely goal it is."

"When you say that, Mamako, I think I might just make this job change work. But don't let me keep you! …Hey, everyone! Mamako's party, coming through!"

And at the Maman Village elder's call...

The villagers nearby began calling out to those ahead of them, and the crowd parted to let them pass.

"We heard you'd yet to reregister from... Er, what was her name...? The admin dressed as a nun. Go on, no time to waste!"

"Such a help. Thank you, elder. Ma-kun, let's go!"

"Yeah, move out!"

Bobbing their heads in gratitude to the helpful villagers, the party surged ahead. Masato was at the lead—and Wise quietly grabbed the spot next to him.

"I was thinking—if Shiraaase's meddling in anything, it's probably *this*."

"Yeah. Seems like the sort of thing she'd do."

They glanced up at the sky, as if her smirking face were staring back at them from above. ""Gone, but not forgotten."" Rest in peace, Shiraaase. (They're joking.)

It didn't take long before they hit another crowd.

The road was completely blocked, but just up ahead—they spotted a man in professorial robes, a good three heads taller than everyone else.

"That's...Mr. Burly! It's been ages!" Medhi called out.

The big man turned around and gave them all a broad grin. Their former teacher, in the flesh. "Oh, Cleric Medhi! Fancy meeting you here! Hero Masato, Sage Wise, Traveling Merchant Porta, and Mamako! Glad to see you all doing well."

"I learned so much in your class. Are you here to reregister, Mr. Burly? Or are you changing jobs?"

"Bwa-ha-ha! I'm a teacher for life; that's the only way for me! My beloved pupils and I just need to keep soldiering on! ...Come, students. Group activity time! Remember what we practiced? Put it in action!"

At his order, the uniformed students formed two rows, one boys, one girls—all with their back to the party. When Mr. Burly blew his whistle, they stepped neatly to either side, opening a path.

Then they all turned around, smiling warmly.

With real faces—no longer ASCII art.

"W-wow…they finally finished your students!"

"That they did! They all have individuality now! I've long wanted to show them off to you, Cleric Medhi, and at last that moment has arrived! I'm so glad Ms. Shiraaase got in touch. Go on, no time like the present."

"Certainly. Thank you very much. Masato, this way."

"Yep."

They moved on, basking in the smiles of their former classmates. "Yo! How's it been?" "Remember me?" "Of course you do!" "S-sure…" Literally no clue who was who but best to smile and move on.

Medhi was walking next to Masato, her smile rather strained. "I suppose I'll have to thank Ms. Shiraaase for this later."

"I guess…"

They glanced up at the sky, as if her smug face were staring back at them. ""Gone, but not forgotten."" Joking, of course. She's probably not dead.

It wasn't much farther before they saw the convention center up ahead. The grounds outside were packed, but once again they spied familiar faces.

Adventurers in intimidating gear—with their mothers. All working to ensure people could move in and out. Only mildly scary.

"Hey, Porta, lemme put you on my shoulders. See if you can tell who that guy in the middle is."

"Okay! Hngg…that mohawk definitely belongs to…Pocchi!"

"Figured. Should we skip to the end?"

"Sure!"

Masato and Porta glanced up at the sky. Shiraaase looked caught off guard and slightly frazzled. "Gone…" "But not forgotten!" Probably not dead. Odds were against it. Still…

Like Porta's Appraise said, the mohawk in the crowd belonged to the roustabout Pocchi. He was here with his mom. All the roustabouts and roustabouts' moms were members of Mom's Guild.

Pocchi caught sight of the party and waved. "You're finally here! Quit dillydallying! Book it! Loads of people've already registered!"

"There's so much we need to catch up on, but this is hardly the time. Go on in! ...Ah, but if you just have one minute, Mamako?"

"Oh, I'm sure we can spare that much..."

Pocchi's mom and Mamako made eye contact. The roustabouts' moms soon gathered round.

If they started chatting here, they'd be talking until the sun went down.

"Wise! Medhi! Grab one arm each! Emergency!"

"Roger!"

"Come, Mamako. Time to go."

"Oh my!"

The girls dragged her off into the grounds beyond. Whew.

Careful not to drop Porta, Masato hurried after them—or started to, but he drew up short.

He had to ask.

"...Pocchi, you were trying to become a childcare worker, right?"

"Eh? Yeah, but I ain't changing jobs. I mean business! You gotta achieve your dreams on your own."

"I can see that..."

"Least, that's how I do it. Not worth the time you spent askin'! Get in there, bozo!"

"Sure! Bye."

This time Masato dashed off—his lips pursed tight, not saying a word. Porta leaned over his head, looking puzzled.

"Masato, is something on your mind?"

"Yeah, but it's not...like, a huge deal. Just...about jobs and stuff. Sooner or later, I'm gonna... Nah, never mind."

"Hm...?"

In front of them lay the chaos of the job fair. Game jobs. Nothing more.

Except...

Jobs, huh...?

For just a moment, a fuzzy notion of his future danced across his mind.

But it was too out of focus to make out.

Masato and Porta finally made it inside the convention hall. There was quite a crowd inside, but they could at least keep things moving.

"Oh, there's Mama!"

"Hey, Mom! Wait up!"

"Oh, Ma-kun, Porta. Over here!"

Mamako was waving at them by the side of the door.

Just her.

"Where's Wise and Medhi?" Masato asked her.

"They're off reregistering. It'd be such a shame if they didn't make it in time, after all. There's so many people here, we might never find each other again, so we promised to meet up at the Mom Shop later. Does that sound good?"

"Very." Masato set Porta down and looked around.

It was definitely a job fair. The whole convention center was partitioned off in rows of booths.

Each booth had a sign with a job name over it, and rows of applicants forming in front. Reregistering or transferring were both completed the moment the paperwork was handed in. The lines were moving steadily.

"Sure are a lot of jobs out there...like, too many. Some of these aren't even jobs."

It wasn't just adventuring jobs (like warrior or mage) or even villager or city folk. They even had booths for elves, beastkin, angels, and devils. Everything you could think of. A glance out the window showed a booth for giants outside.

Porta spotted some familiar mothers in line at the fantasy race booths. "Oh, the mothers from the World Matriarchal Arts Tournament are here!"

"The bug affected the other server, too? ...And all because of my mom?"

"We'll have to say hello later. But first..."

"Yeah, gotta reregister ourselves."

"Right! I'll be back soon!" Porta bowed and turned to run off.

"Oh, wait, Porta. Before you go, can I grab a resurrection item?"

"Sure! No problem. But who's it for?"

"The gone-but-not-forgotten lady." Masato was looking at the center of the hall, where a huge sign said HERO.

Despite the crowds, no one was going near it—but there *was* a single coffin.

He gave Porta a quick boost so she could see. "Go get her, Masato!"

"On it." He took the revival jewel from her, and she ran off toward the Traveling Merchant booth.

Now then.

"I'm heading over. Mom?"

"I'm coming with you! Mommy's already registered."

"You're just sticking with 'Ma-kun's Mommy,' then? Fine, have it your way. We're off."

"Let's go!"

Masato and Mamako headed for the Hero booth. His priority was clear—he had to take care of that coffin.

When he used the revival item, the coffin vanished...and the mysterious nun—who it turned out really had been dead after all—was back on her feet.

"Well, well. Masato, Mamako—short time no see."

"Barely minutes. Why are you here?"

"I just had to see if you were enjoying my little scheme. The moment I saw you off, I used admin protocols to warp myself to the employee entrance. And the crowds were so suffocating, I accidentally died, successfully achieving my quota."

"You never miss a beat, Ms. Shiraaase. Hee-hee."

"You have a quota for showing up dead? What use is that?"

"It is the Shiraaase special. Now then..." She took a quick glance around, thinking.

"What's wrong?"

"I was looking for someone. I imagined he would be here soon... Oh, there he is."

Masato turned to look and saw someone walking toward them.

A huge sword on his back. Quite handsome. He was pushing through the crowds, apologizing to anyone he bumped into on the way.

Masato knew that face—they'd met during the Catharn garbage disaster.

"Hawk! How you been?"

"Hey, Masato. We meet again."

. Hawk had finally reached the Hero booth. He and Masato bumped fists.

Then…

"Oh, lovely! You're back again, dear."

Mamako sounded a bit too friendly, and Hawk hastily backed off.

"H-hello, Mamako! Long time no see. I am an adventurer named Hawk! Once again, I am here as part of my professional duties."

"Oh my, that's right. You're Hawk again today. Hee-hee-hee."

She seemed weirdly delighted, and Hawk was clearly sweating it, but they wound up grinning at each other.

This was clearly suspicious.

"Goodness, your scarf is out of place! Let me fix that for you, dear."

"Oh, is it? Thank you. Please do. And call me Hawk."

Mamako was now fussing over him as if she'd done it many times before.

As if she was fixing her husband's tie.

Masato had seen her do this at home many times, and the resemblance was striking.

"Okay, I gotta ask…do you two know each other?"

"N-no? I first met Mamako during the uproar the other day—"

"We've known each other since before you were born, Ma-kun. Back when Mommy was in junior college! We met in a seminar there."

"Don't…!"

"Oh, really? That long, huh? And gosh, that sure sounds like the story of how you got married." Masato glared at Hawk.

Hawk failed to meet his eye.

"…Hawk."

"Y-yes, Masato?"

"I can think of only one person my mom calls 'dear.'"

"R-really? That's, uh… Ha-ha. Ha."

Hawk's eyes were darting all over the place. He was floundering. One more push would finish him off. Masato readied the fatal blow…!

But before he could slam it home, someone held out a piece of paper in front of him. His job application.

"Sorry to interrupt," said Shiraaase, "but you should handle your reregistration first."

"Y-yes, Masato! Do as Shiraaase says. That's what's important here!"

"Tch. I knew you two were in cahoots."

"I have no idea what you mean. I'll get Hawk registered, so you two fill out everything on this form. Starting with your name."

"Yeah, yeah, I can read. Geez." Masato had plenty more to gripe about, but first things first.

He slammed the application down on the table and got to filling it out. Hawk gingerly took up the space next to him.

Masato began by scribbling his name at the top...

"Incidentally, I can infooorm you the top of the application is for administrative use. Your name goes in the field below. Not your real name, but the name you use *in-game*. Don't get it wrong."

""Huh?""

Too late. Masato had already written Masato Oosuki at the very top. Hawk had also let out a yelp.

Hayato Oosuki

His real name...was in the wrong field, too.

"...Aha!" Masato said, spotting Hawk's application. Frowning, he fixed the boy with his best glare.

"Same mistake, huh? I guess blood is thicker than water. Ha-ha-ha," said Hawk, his smile so bright it took the wind out of Masato's sails.

And in the job field...Hawk had written Demon Lord.

What the heck? It took Masato a moment to process...

Then Hawk took the sword off his back and slammed the tip into the ground. A whirlwind sprang up around it.

"Yo! What are you doing? Argh!"

"Oh my! We don't want you flying away, Ma-kun. Let Mommy hold on to you."

"Definitely helps!"

Mamako had a grip on his clothes, and that was all that was keeping him in place.

The hall was instantly plunged into chaos. The partitions dividing the booths as well as the people waiting in line were all blown away. A certain someone was back in her coffin.

Three figures forced their way through the gales: Porta in the lead, with Wise and Medhi right behind.

"Masato! Mama! Are you okay?"

"Yeah, we're fine!"

"And so are you girls! Thank goodness."

"Yep. So what the heck's going on here?"

"What caused this sudden tornado?"

"Ask him," Masato said, rather annoyed. "His real name's Hayato Oosuki. Forty-two years old. Said this was for work, so he disguised himself as an adventurer our age and called himself Hawk—but he's actually my dad."

As if he'd been waiting for these words, the winds died down—and the man at the eye of the hurricane appeared.

He wore a jacket like Masato's gear—but clearly of higher quality.

And his blade was twice the size of Firmamento. A cursed greatsword as black as outer space—Universo.

Ruggedly handsome features, gazing down at Masato like a father would.

Demon Lord Hayato.

"Now I can finally speak as myself—as your Demon Lord Dad."

"As my what? You are *way* too old to be a Demon Lord. Why are you even here? I thought the whole reason you aren't living with us is because your current job posting is *so* important!"

"This is *for* that same job. I said I was here in a professional capacity! I agreed to become the Demon Lord as a parent—as a father—and because the job must be done."

"Suuuure… And what kinda job is *that*? Why are you here?"

Hayato might be his dad, but he was calling himself a Demon Lord, and that blade's aura was gnarly. Masato was on edge, his hand on the hilt of his holy sword.

And the Demon Lord's job…

"First, I must apologize."

"Huh?"

Hayato swung around and bowed his head low to the trembling crowd.

"Good citizens, I apologize for inciting panic!"

A genuine, heartfelt apology.

"Uh, wait...Dad?"

"When your actions inconvenience others, you apologize. Perfectly normal! I would be ashamed to do anything else with my son watching. Next..."

The Demon Lord moved to the nearest partitions and began setting them back in place. Clearly planning to put the whole venue back the way it was.

Masato stood there blinking until Mamako slapped him on the back.

"Come, Ma-kun. We can't let the Demon Lord do all the work!"

"We can't?"

The girls each slapped his back, too.

"You're the Hero, and we're the Hero's party. We gotta help, too!"

"When you think about it, this is a boss battle. We must emerge victorious."

"Masato! Let's help!"

"I...guess?"

"Ah-ha! Banding together with your friends to defeat me? Very well. No decent Demon Lord would back down now!"

"Then it's a battle! Woo!"

"W-woo?"

Demon Lord Hayato vs the Hero's Party—FIGHT!

Mamako and Porta boldly assembled partitions.

Wise and Medhi used their polished skills to put the long tables back in place.

"Keep it up, everyone! Just keep knocking them out!"

""""Yeah!"""""

This was working. Slow and steady. The hall was starting to look like its old self—their approach was effective.

But they couldn't get comfortable. An attack was inbound!

"You're the ones responsible for this?! Do you have any idea how busy we are?!"

"How dare you! We're in a hurry!"

Complaints from the registration staff, and glares from the job fair attendees, rained down upon them.

These attacks could not be evaded—they could only be parried with sincerity.

Demon Lord Hayato and Hero Masato stood side-by-side, backs straight, waists bent, heads bowed!

"I cannot apologize enough! You too, son!"

"I'm deeply sorry... Wait, I didn't do anything wrong! What's even going on here?!"

But protesting the injustice did not get him anywhere. There was no mercy in war.

Who would be the first to grow weary, and take a knee? The Demon Lord, or the Hero?

The battle raged on!

The sun had set—it was now night.

The job fair meant every inn in town was packed, and it took quite a trek before the party found a place to stay. The baffling battle had worn them all out, and they all dragged their feet on the way to the dining hall.

Tonight's dinner was hamburger steaks accompanied by a nutritious soup and salad.

"All the cleanup's done, and everyone's registered! Isn't that nice? Put your hands together! What do we say before a meal?"

""""""""Thanks for the food!""""""""

They were seated at a round table, their faces stuffed with a mother's good cooking, all their fatigue having vanished.

"I made a lot, so feel free to ask for seconds!"

Their appetites brought Mamako no end of pleasure.

"I definitely need more than usual today!" chirped Porta.

"You can't end a day without a Mamako meal," said Wise. "Sooo good!"

"Oh dear. I can't stop myself from eating more...," said Medhi.

Porta was next to Mamako, Wise next to Porta, and Medhi next to Wise—all of them smiling, too.

Next to Medhi was Shiraaase—who was keeping her expression serene, but smiling on the inside.

And next to her...

"On my previous visit, time was short and I missed out on joining you for dinner. Getting to eat Mamako's cooking again is all the joy a man could wish for. I'm so happy, I could cry."

...the Demon Lord Hayato was *also* smiling.

The whole table was all smiles!

Except for Masato, who was seated on the other side of the Demon Lord. He was looking kinda sullen.

"Why are the Hero and Demon Lord sharing a meal? Does nobody see a problem here?"

"Masato, can I ask something?"

"Go ahead, Wise."

"What the heck's a Demon Lord anyway?"

"That's what I wanna know! Ask him! Actually, no, I'll do it." Masato let out a long, exasperated sigh, then turned toward Hayato. "Dad, what are you even doing?"

"Sharing dinner with you. What else?"

"But that's weird! You're the Demon Lord, right? So why are you here eating with the rest of us? ...I mean, I hate to suggest it, but shouldn't you be out doing evil stuff? Like terrorizing the world or something...?"

"Ha-ha-ha, I wouldn't do that. True, I'm a Demon Lord, but only in a very specific way. My role is in opposition to the Hero—you, my son. I came to this world to exert my paternal influence upon you."

"Uh, I'm not following."

"Hm, how do I put this, then...? For certain reasons, I can't explain all the details to you right off the bat, but...well, let's put it like this: I'm here to test you. Kind of like an exam proctor."

"So just...call yourself that, then?"

"Fair, but this is no ordinary test... To complete my mission, I'll need to be a bit ruthless. I must be ready to wield powers against those who matter to me most. I might even be called upon to earn Mama-ko's wrath."

"Her wrath? …You think Mom would ever get seriously mad at you?"

Masato gave his mother a searching look, but she was just blinking at them. He wasn't sure if she was shaken or simply not following the conversation.

Hayato saw this and mustered a half smile.

"Consider this Demon Lord title my way of shouldering a burden. Still, it's high time I took my leave of you. There is much I must take care of back in the real world before the day is out. I'll see you all again tomorrow morning."

"Oh my! You're that busy? When will you be back? Should I have breakfast ready?"

"I would love nothing more…but I'm afraid I can't promise I'd make it here in time."

"Hee-hee. You and Ma-kun are both such sleepyheads, after all!"

"My alarm clock always wakes me up to the sound of my beloved wife's voice. It's so comforting that I end up drifting right back to sleep—an unfortunate side effect. Good-bye, everyone."

With that very "married couple" interaction complete, the Demon Lord left the dining hall.

And thus…

Masato found everyone looking at him.

"…Wh-what?"

"Nothing!" Wise retorted. "Just…like father, like son."

"I feel like I should object to that comment on principle… And why is it none of you seem surprised that Hawk was really my dad?"

"I sort of had a feeling the whole time!" said Porta.

"You did?!"

"Same here. Just, like…a hunch. Plus he was trying real hard to hide it."

"And that was a dead giveaway. He's exactly who I would expect your father to be… *Giggle…*"

"Hey, what's that supposed to mean, Medhi? Are you calling us idiots?"

"You really do take after him, especially when you're hiding something. The way you two make excuses—it's exactly the same. I always know right away. Hee-hee-hee."

"Mom! You're supposed to have *our* backs!"

Masato was alone in the world. How sad.

But then...

"Tsk, tsk. Demon Lord Hayato left without infooorming you of the most important thing! Like he was leaving that task to me—as my name is Shiraaase, and *Shiraaase* means 'infooorm.'"

There was steak sauce all over the mysterious nun's lips, but she wiped it away and leaned forward. "Now, everyone—there is something else you should know about the test Masato must undergo."

"What? Is this a big thing? That requires mad exposition? Wait, the admins are involved?"

"A big, resounding 'Yes!' to all those questions."

"She didn't even try denying it," said Wise.

Shiraaase had thrown out a thumbs-up so hard, it glittered. Moving right along:

"Let me make it official: The Demon Lord quest, administered by Demon Lord Hayato, has now begun. This quest is specifically for you, Masato."

"Oh, fantastic. Can't wait to hear it."

"I love the enthusiasm. In a sense, this quest is purely a private matter for the Oosuki family...but like it or not, Mamako and the rest of your party will inevitably get dragged into your mess."

"Your phrasing leaves much to be desired," said Medhi, "but I'd be happy to help."

"Same here! Masato helped with my mommy, so I want to help him!"

"*Sniff*, what a sweet child!" said Wise. "So, Shiraaase. What's the deal with this Demon Lord quest?"

"You'll find out once it begins! Heh. Heh. Heh."

"Yep, saw that coming," said Masato.

Shiraaase's smirk was super sus. Everyone knew that meant bad news.

But this quest was personally tailored for Masato. How could he refuse? He'd overcome countless trials, resolved many family prob-lems. He was the heroic son—this was his duty.

And he knew full well he hadn't done any of that on his own.

"Just like always, we'll figure it out together. As a party..."

"And as mother and son. Right, Ma-kun?"

"Exactly."

He held out a hand, and Mamako put hers on it—and the girls' hands on top of that.

"We started with Wise, then Medhi, then Porta—and finally, it's my turn. We'll clear this Daddy Demon Lord quest, and solve our party's parent dilemma once and for all. Ready? Then let's—"

"Let's all do our best! Woo!"

""""Woo!""""

"Mom, can you please just once... Oh, never mind."

This was how it always went. Just as he was getting fired up, she jumped in. And that meant they'd pull it off again. He was confident—and his party looked just as sure of themselves.

Shiraaase watched them all, smiling warmly. "The bonds of the strongest parent and child... Let's hope that strength does not prove your undoing."

No one present heard that ominous whisper.

Parent and Child Awareness Survey
Adventurer Final Exam Vol. 1

Are you close to your mother?
Close enough to fight, I guess.

Do you talk with your mother? How often?
It's more screaming than talking, but...yeah, pretty often.

Has your mother said anything lately that made you happy?
Nothing specific, but now she actually looks at me when I talk to her, which is kinda nice.

Has your mother said anything lately that made you unhappy?
Wish she'd shut up about my boobs.

Do you ever go shopping with your mother?
I'd go if she asked. (But we're living in different worlds right now.)

Do you help your mother?
I make her let me. (She sucks at housework, so I gotta do everything.)

What does your mother like?
Slim, wiry builds and pretty faces.

What does your mother hate?
Anything that requires effort.

What are your mother's strong points?
Her hands-off approach.

What are your mother's weak points?
Her brain.

If you went on an adventure with your mom, would you become closer?
A lot happened, but I guess the upshot was we did get closer.

Answers: Wise

Chapter 2 Don't Accept the Demon Lord's Invitation! ...But I Guess Refusing Is Rude Sometimes.

The next morning.

To prepare for the Demon Lord Hayato's arrival, they had an early breakfast and were waiting in the dining hall.

"...Dad's kinda late, huh?"

Masato forced his head up off the table, stealing another look out the window.

When their vigil had started, they could still see the morning sun— but it had long since cleared the window frame.

The whole party were sick of waiting.

Wise had her head on the table and wasn't moving. Medhi had killed some time by brushing her hair, but her patented beautiful girl smile had taken on a distinctively grumpy note. She was taking it out on Wise, dismantling her trademark curly pigtails. Porta was fast asleep.

Mamako had gone off to the kitchen, and now she came back with even more tea.

Nobody was thirsty. Except Shiraaase, who chugged hers. "Ahhh... He's definitely a bit *too* late. Perhaps we shouldn't expect him at all."

"Yeah... Geez, Dad, get it together."

"I wonder if he overslept like you did, Ma-kun."

"Don't lump me in with him! Anyway, if it's gonna be like this, Shiraaase..."

"Very well. I have been briefed on the particulars of the Demon Lord quest, so I might as well give you a rundown."

And she rose to her feet.

Following her lead, they left the inn.

The Catharn convention center was still in the throes of the job fair.

The streets were less packed than the day before but still teeming. The party was forced to surf the flow and exit the stream at a side street.

They were headed for the Mom Shop, a small café-like store. This was a facility that solved family problems and had become their base of operations.

"What are we doing here?" Masato asked Shiraaase.

"Nothing, really. I just thought you should be aware of what's going on."

"Meaning...?"

Shiraaase didn't answer—she just headed inside.

The bell on the door tinkled, and a girl's head popped up from behind the counter. She was the Dark God in charge of spoiling and the sole employee of the Mom Shop—Mone.

"Oh, Ms. Shiraaase! Welcome."

"Good morning, Mone. Sorry to intrude."

"Not a problem! Make yourself at home."

Mone greeted Shiraaase with aplomb, but the moment her eyes lit on Masato's party...

"Oh, customers? How lovely to meet you! Welcome to the Mom Shop!"

"......Huh?"

Weird way to greet people she knew. And that smile of hers just screamed customer service.

Mone usually greeted Masato by throwing her arms around him and rubbing her cheek on his chest to refuel her spoil meter.

"Uh, Mone? What's going on?"

"Er...why do you know my name?"

"Huh?"

"Hmm?"

They blinked at each other for a minute.

"Ugh, both of you, quit goofing off. This is hardly the time for that."

"Mone, I think this prank has gone on long enough."

"Um, uh, what? I'm not pulling a prank..."

Wise and Medhi were just making Mone even warier.

Only one solution. Masato pushed Porta forward. A purity attack would make it impossible for anyone to pretend to be a stranger.

"Um, Mone! It's me! Porta! Do you not remember me?"

"Er, sorry. Have we met?"

Even Porta's pure gaze had failed.

"Then it's time for our last resort. Mom, take it from here!"

"Very well. Mone, it's me. You know who I am, don't you?"

"*Gasp!* I can sense infinite spoiling!"

Mone's arms went up, ready to wrap around Mamako—but she stopped herself, backing away. She hid behind the counter, like a wild animal suspecting a trap.

She seemed to genuinely not know who they were.

"Shiraaase, what's going on?"

"Allow me to explain. Mone, I apologize for alarming you. We'll be going now."

"S-sure. Come again..."

Outside the Mom Shop, Shiraaase began strolling leisurely up the street. The others followed her.

There were still quite a few people around, but nobody spared them a second glance. Mamako's swaying bosom attracted a few stares— resulting in some red-faced men—but that was it.

A housewife with a shopping basket crossed the path in front of them. Without even glancing in Mamako's direction.

"Mommy knows that lady..."

"Seriously? And she didn't stop to chat? You've gotta be kidding me!" said Masato. "That's just like how Mone didn't seem to know who we are... Then that means... Shiraaase!"

He felt a tug at his heartstrings.

Shiraaase paused and turned back, nodding. "I can infooorm you that with the start of the Demon Lord quest, all NPCs in the world have had their memories of you sealed."

"Sealed memories, huh? I figured."

"Wait, Masato, how does that make sense?"

"Ms. Shiraaase, could you please explain why their memories are sealed?" asked Medhi.

"The reason... Well, I'll leave that to the exam proctor."

They could hear rapid footsteps approaching them from behind.

The Demon Lord Hayato. His greatsword and jacket under one arm, his bedhead flouncing around as he ran.

"Oh! Masato's daddy!" said Porta.

"Goodness, the sleepyhead's finally joined us," said Mamako.

"S-sorry! The meeting last night went a bit late, and I didn't get to bed until— *Cough cough!*"

As he caught up with them, he crumpled to the ground, his breathing coming in gasps. "Oof, I'm gonna feel that in my legs tomorrow…" How very middle-aged.

His heroic son couldn't bear to watch. "Dad, please… Could you try to be a *little* more Demon Lord-y?"

"I—I'll try… Whew… Okay."

"Dear, you stay right there. You can't be a proper Demon Lord with your hair like that!"

"Oh, thanks. Please."

Mamako kept him on his knees and began fussing with his bedhead. "I've got a brush." "Porta, do you have a spritzer?" "I do!" Wise, Medhi, and Porta all chipped in as an impromptu hair and makeup team. They even put his jacket on and greatsword on his back.

The Demon Lord had returned.

With Mamako at his side, Wise, Medhi, and Porta close by, and even Shiraaase right behind, Hayato turned to the Hero, Masato.

"Mwa-ha-ha-ha! We meet again, my heroic son!"

"Uh, you're kind of in my spot, but whatever."

"Moving right along, if I could just address the itinerary for the day—"

"We've already been briefed. It's a Demon Lord–supervised quest, right? You left without explaining it, so Shiraaase covered for you."

"Sh-she did?!"

The Demon Lord turned toward Shiraaase and gave her a polite bow. "I do apologize. That was entirely my shortcoming." "Not at all." "Can you not keep the Demon Lord act up for two seconds?" Masato demanded. This was an especially humble Demon Lord.

After taking a moment to recover:

"Well, Masato, anything you wish to say to your dad?" Hayato asked.

"Sure. Why have all the NPCs had their memories of us sealed? Start there."

"Very well! It's quite simple, really. You and your party have done so much, and people across the world have recognized you for your efforts. But that works against the test. So we sealed their memories."

"Works against it how…?"

"I'm here to test the power you have, Masato—the power to progress toward the future."

As for what that was supposed to mean:

"It's nothing particularly complicated. Typical stuff, really. For instance, say you had amazing grades at school."

"S-sure."

"But if you moved on to college, or got a job—found yourself in a new environment—what would happen to you? Everything would be different. You wouldn't know a soul. Nobody would have a clue what you've accomplished. You'd have to start all over from square one. You'd have to progress from that point."

"So I need this power you speak of?"

"And as your father, I merely want to know if you have it. That's why the test must be done where nobody knows your party. Well? Do you have the courage to give this a try?"

The Demon Lord shot Masato a daring wink. Granted, the wink was coming from a forty-something-year-old man.

Masato rolled his eyes, but took the question seriously.

The future…

The thought had crossed his mind at the job fair.

A future he couldn't quite picture—did he have the power to move toward it?

Might as well give it a try.

"Sounds worth it. Let's find out!" He gave Hayato his best grin.

"That settles it, then. Let's head to the Adventurers Guild. That's where the quest begins! …And Masato…"

"What?"

"This may be a game, but everything you experience here is real. Don't let that reality get you down."

With that ominous utterance, the Demon Lord turned to leave, the girls in his wake.

Masato followed them.

"Okay, seriously, why are you all sticking by *him*? That makes no sense!"

Nobody paid this any heed. He was alone.

But he wouldn't let it get to him. He had to proceed toward the future!

"Don't worry, Ma-kun. Mommy will always be with you."

"Gah, when did you get there?"

Mamako had her arms tightly around his, cradling him in the valley of her bosoms.

The party reached the guild.

"Well, Masato," said the Demon Lord. "Pick any quest you like, whatever looks good to you."

"Lemme see...uh..."

"Oh, Ma-kun! What about this one? It says 'gather seasonal ingredients'!"

"That's what *you* want to do."

Mamako was still clinging to him as they scoped out the quest board.

Not far away, the Demon Lord was doing the same thing. The girls and Shiraaase were at his side, waiting.

"Yo, Shiraaase is one thing, but why are you all over there? Are you trying to make a point? Come back already!"

"We could do that, but...your dad's going on about how he wants to test your ability to manage on your own, right?" said Wise.

"If we're with you, wouldn't that get in the way?" suggested Medhi.

"Okay, good point. But still...I know someone who doesn't seem concerned about all that..."

He gave Mamako a pointed look, but she not only failed to let go of his arm, she grinned. She definitely had no plans to leave his side. Demon Lord Hayato was stifling a laugh.

"You in the same boat, Porta?" Masato asked.

"S-sorry! I think your daddy could tell me things about my mommy's work, so I'm gonna stay over here!"

"Huh? Why would Dad know about Deathmother?"

"I can infooorm you there is nothing unusual about that. Hayato is a business-side consultant working with this game's management division and regularly meets with admin reps."

"...Huh?" Masato gaped at Shiraaase, but she didn't bat an eye. He turned and gave the Demon Lord the same stare.

"News to you?" Hayato said, sounding proud of himself. "Maybe you'll take a little more interest in your father's work from now on!"

"This is *real*?"

"That it is! But just to be clear, I'm not involved in test player selection or the actual running of the game itself. My involvement is purely on the business end of things. I was aware that the two of you were involved, but that's all."

"I'll admit your relationship to Hayato did play a minor role in your selection. Heh-heh-heh." Shiraaase chuckled.

"Shiraaase...I really wish you would stop sharing all our behind-the-scenes secrets...," said Demon Lord Hayato.

Masato elected to ignore the uncomfortable facts. "You knew, Mom?"

"I heard he was in charge of something very important, but I didn't know it was this game. Mommy's very surprised."

"Yeah, same here..."

The game they were playing, *MMMMMORPG* (working title), was sponsored by the Japanese government. It was headed toward a nationwide rollout. And not only was Masato's father involved, he was working at an executive level.

"Dad, are you, like...actually a big shot?"

"Ha-ha-ha! Good question."

His father just laughed it off. This Demon Lord was powerful in more ways than one.

"Picked out your quest yet?" Hayato asked. "I've already chosen mine. I'll be over here, accepting it."

"Go right ahead. I won't be long."

"Is that a newfound note of respect in your voice?"

"Kinda, I guess?"

Masato turned back to the board and grabbed the quest he'd been eyeing. Then he followed Hayato to the counter.

The Demon Lord went first, handing the receptionist the quest card. "I'd like to accept this quest, if you would be so kind."

"Exterminating monsters on the main road? Who'll be joining you?"

The three girls behind Hayato—Wise, Medhi, and Porta—all raised their hands. Shiraaase began coughing like she had consumption, stepping away. Obviously not joining in.

Clear on the party size, the receptionist turned her gaze back to Hayato.

"In that case—*Ultimate Art: Receptionist Search!* Hnggg!"

This was a strict eyeing-up that allowed her to determine if he qualified for this quest.

Top-tier gear, balanced physique, the confidence earned through years of high-level job experience, and the maturity his age provided...

The receptionist's scan complete, she nodded. "You seem trustworthy. I'll accept your request. Good luck out there!"

"Thank you."

Demon Lord Hayato's quest was approved.

Next, Masato. He handed the posting over. "Hi there. I'd like this one."

"Exterminate the midsized dragon in the dungeon near town. And joining you..."

"Hello!" Mamako said, waving—still pressed up against her son. "Mommy's with her Ma-kun."

"Right. And since Shiraaase didn't join Dad—"

"Negatory. I'm afraid I can accompany neither party. I must prepare for the next phase."

"'Phase'?"

"Ahem. Pay that no heed. If you'll excuse me..."

She turned and hustled off. Clearly up to something. Something no good.

And thus, Masato's party was left at two.

The receptionist gave both of them a scan and frowned. "Just the two of you? I'm afraid this might be rather difficult..."

"Nah, it'll be fine. We may not look it, but we're pretty good. We've cleared quests like this before."

"Inexperienced adventurers love to make these claims..."

"I swear it's true! Go ahead and do a proper check—you'll see!"

"Well, if you insist... *Receptionist Search! Hngg.*"

She seemed highly unenthused, but gave him a once-over nonetheless.

Not bad equipment, properly growing physique, the vigor of youth, face still pretty boyish...

Her check complete, the receptionist gave him her best smile. "Choose something else."

"Whaaa...? No, wait! You can't judge me on looks! C'mon, check my stats! You'll know how good we really are!"

"No need. As a seasoned receptionist, I can gauge anyone's abilities at a glance. Heh."

"And I'm telling you, you're not doing that at all!! ...Damn, starting without anyone knowing us is tougher than I thought. Do I really look that pathetic?!"

"Regardless, for the two of you, I'd say... Yes, this quest would be more appropriate. What do you think?"

She handed over a quest posting.

It said...

About halfway between the Catharn capital and the school town, Mahweh.

What should have been a safe thoroughfare was teeming with bears, wolves, and giant insects. The moment these monsters saw a human, they roared so loud, their bodies vibrated—it was very intimidating.

But the Demon Lord Hayato's party didn't flinch.

"Oh? Are those dragons I spy? ...No matter; let's make quick work of them. Everybody ready?"

"You bet, Masato's dad! My ultimate magic will knock 'em dead!"

"Porta, ready items to cure magic seal. It's highly likely Wise's magic is already sealed, and she merely has failed to notice."

"You got it! Here!"

"I'm not sealed! Medhi, don't even joke about this!"

"Ha-ha-ha, as lively as you are lovely. That's what adventures are all about… Off I go!"

Hayato darted forward, the cursed greatsword Universo in one hand, making a sweeping slash.

The air before him split asunder, revealing the universe underneath. Incredibly tiny meteors shot out from the tear in space like incendiary arrows.

The moment they hit their targets, the meteors exploded—again, and again, and again. Like they'd been carpet-bombed, the monster pack was annihilated.

The girls stood stunned.

"Uh, Masato's dad? You're hella broken…"

"The power of the universe… It's essentially an upgraded version of the Heavens. We really shouldn't let Masato see this." *Glance.*

"Masato's daddy is really strong! Just like Mama!"

"Am I? That's nice to hear. Let's keep it up! Come on, everyone!"

""""Okay!""""

Demon Lord Hayato was a born leader. The girls tagged along, and the four of them made swift work of any foes.

And while they were getting super into it…

Over here…

"Argh…Medhi totally knew I could hear her…"

"Oh my. Ma-kun, your hands stopped!"

Masato and Mamako were picking weeds by the side of the road. This was the quest the receptionist had chosen for them.

Masato was ready to cry.

"I…I can bring down a meteor or two…if I *really* want to! I can do spectacle fighting! I just haven't yet. But I *could! Sniff.*"

"Ma-kun, if you feel like crying, come right over here to my chest. Mommy will hold you close."

"Yeah, no thanks."

He wiped the tears with his quest-issued gardening gloves and glanced again at the Demon Lord's party.

Hayato was mowing monsters down, and Medhi was swinging her staff with her best cover girl smile, beating monsters to death.

Porta was hastily opening her shoulder bag and curing Wise, who was using her tome as a pillow, taking a sulk nap.

"One of the monsters released a shock wave when it roared... She had her magic sealed before the fight even began. Now that takes talent," said Masato.

He considered making fun of her for it, but...figured she'd just turn it back on him.

He glanced down at the fistful of weeds he'd pulled, and sighed.

"Ma-kun, go on," Mamako suddenly whispered.

"Go where?"

"Leave the weeding to Mommy. I can always wrap this up with the Holy Sword of Earth if I have to. So you go do what you want to do, Ma-kun. Have fun!"

"Mom...!"

Everyone should have a mother this kind. Masato was filled with joy and gratitude.

He almost jumped to his feet...

"...Nah, better not."

...but knelt back down and focused on the weeds at hand.

"Ma-kun? Are you sure?"

"Yeah. I am."

"Is this that thing where you don't want my help?" *Sniff.*

"Nah. It's not that thing. It's just—*this* is my job right now."

He was acting calm, but there was a fierce debate going on within.

Naturally, he wanted to go fight. Cut loose with all his friends. Abandon this grunt work and enjoy himself. Deep down, that's what he really wanted.

But he thought doing that would be conceding defeat.

I feel like this is exactly what Dad's trying to test.

Obviously, he felt stupid taking this so seriously. But he really didn't want to give in.

So Masato sucked it up and attacked the weeds in front of him.

"I said I'd do this. So I'm gonna finish it. I want Dad to know I'm a man of my word. Show him I've grown up, y'know."

"Ma-kun...! How mature! *Sniff!*" His mother was moved to tears!

"Yeah, yeah, don't cry. Quit goofing off and let's get this done."

"Hee-hee. Fair. The sooner we're done...the sooner you can go!"

"Exactly! I can join the fray with my head held high."

He still had an impatient childish side. To help him focus, he turned his back on the Demon Lord's party. Work was work. He loved work.

Hayato's party were staring at Masato's back.

"Masato's really hanging in there! Mama looks so happy!"

"I figured he'd give up immediately, but he's actually trying. Pisses me off."

"Since when did he have such impressive willpower? I can't stand it."

"Um, Wise, Medhi? My son's diligently applying himself, so I'm not sure why that's upsetting you..."

"Take it as a compliment," said Wise. "Don't worry about it, Masato's dad."

"Y-you're sure? ...Teens these days with their slang..."

Wise and Medhi did indeed look rather happy. As happy as Hayato was confused.

But when he looked back over at his son, his gaze was gentle—peaceful.

Hayato's party and Masato's party spent a while attacking monsters and weeds, respectively. Tasks completed, they headed back to the Catharn guild.

First order of business: Report back to the receptionist.

"Demon Lord Hayato, good work on your extermination," she said. "It seems the midsized dragon escaped the dungeon and you took it out along with the monsters on the road, so this is your reward."

"Thank you kindly."

A hefty leather bag of coins was dropped into his palm. With the bonus fee, it was clearly over ten thousand mum.

"Next, um...Mamako's son, right?"

"We never even told you Mom's name, so how does that work? ... Don't tell me her presence is loosening the seal on your memories...?"

"Good work on your weeding. Here is your reward."

Masato held out his hand, and a few scant coins were dropped into it. Less than two thousand mum. Hourly wage of a thousand mum each.

Masato glanced sidelong at Hayato's laden pouch, then at the coins in his palm, and really wanted to let that wriggling frustration lash out, but...

"...Nah, this is just a start. Gotta work my way up."

The money they earned meant something. He put it carefully in his pocket. "Hee-hee-hee. Ma-kun." "Oh, right." He handed Mamako her half.

Hayato was grinning at them. "Sorry to strike an early lead. Well, Masato? If the harsh reality of the modern workplace is too much for you, we could call it quits."

"Don't make me laugh. I'm doing just fine. And I'm gonna take something better next time—gonna *make* them let me."

"That's the spirit! Let's find our next quests."

"First, got a sec? I wanna ask you a favor," Wise said, hand raised. Medhi and Porta were with her.

"The three of us would like to change parties."

"I wanna join Masato's side!"

"Oh-ho? No longer playing as the Demon Lord's minions? You'd rather be in the Hero's party again? You've got a lot of nerve."

The Demon Lord shot them a chilling glare, his hand reaching for the hilt of his blade. "Wha?!" "F-for real?" "Eep!" His blade was merciless and brooked no treachery...!

But Hayato himself just smiled. "Excellent suggestion. Do as you please!"

"Er...y-you're sure? Really?"

"Really. All three of you wish to help Masato out, yes?"

"Yes! I want to be useful to him!"

"Watching him work hard like that inevitably led me to that realization."

"Ha-ha-ha...I'll assume that's a compliment. What do you say,

Masato?" Hayato lightly clapped his son on the shoulder. "You earned their change of hearts all on your own. That is to say—"

"You don't have to tell me—this is a reward no money can buy, right? I appreciate it."

"Excellent! Then I shall forfeit your beloved companions."

"Thanks. I only need Porta, though."

He took Porta's hand and headed back to Mamako. "Ow?!" Wise and Medhi had stomped on his feet.

Be that as it may…

The party lineups had shifted. Demon Lord Hayato was on his own, while Masato's side had the full lineup. They once again began poring over the quest board.

"We're ready for anything now! This time I'll get to really strut my stuff. My ultimate magic's gonna knock down everything in its path!"

"Uh-oh!" Porta squeaked. "Wise, the last fight's seal is still active! You can't use magic at all!"

"Wha?"

"I should've left your useless butt on my dad's team."

"Fear not, Masato. Wise may be a lost cause, but you have me. Even if your own abilities are merely a downgraded version of your father's, I will offer you my full support."

"I should've…see above."

"Hee-hee. We do so much better when we're all together! …Oh? Ma-kun, what about this one?"

Mamako picked up a posting and showed it to him.

No, not a posting. A flyer for a grocery sale. "That's not funny!" "Oh, sorry." Moms always know when to throw in a joke.

While they were fussing about, Hayato picked a quest and took it to the counter.

"You can clearly handle this on your own, Demon Lord Hayato. Exterminate the monsters in the mines near Yomamaburg. Do your worst!"

"Always do."

He glanced back at his son with a grin.

Masato wasn't taking that lying down.

"Yeah, yeah, mock me all you want. I'm gonna show you I can earn people's respect on my own!"

Mamako was right behind Masato. Plus he had Wise, Medhi, and Porta by his side. How could he lose?

His competitive spirit ignited, he deliberately sought out a quest in the Yomamaburg area: Eliminate a mystery monster in the sewers beneath the city.

Just to be extra sure, he adjusted his clothes and hair before heading to the counter.

He'd taken that weed-pulling job seriously. But this time...!

"Yeah, yeah, Mamako's son. We've got a job even a noob can do."

"You've gotten ruder?! The heck?!"

She didn't even look at the request. One glance his way, and she slammed a different posting on the counter.

It said...

At the center of a barren wasteland was the merchant town of Yomamaburg, a casino haven full of dazzling lights.

Not far away, at the entrance to the mines, a fierce battle was nearing its end.

"*Hidden Art: Demon Lord Slash!* ...Gosh, that feels silly."

There was a giant snake coiled around the mountain, and Hayato had unleashed a powerful attack that cleaved the head in two. The monster's body turned to dust, which then transformed into gems that glowed like lamps. They rained on the heads of the miners watching from the shadows.

The foreman in charge came running over to the Demon Lord, warm tears gushing down his rugged cheeks. "Thank you! Thank you, kind Demon Lord! You have saved us all!"

"You're quite welcome. Glad to have been of assistance."

"That varmint gobbled up all the gems we use to light the mines and left us high and dry! At last we can get back to work. You've been a big help. Oh, say..."

"Yes?"

"Given your strength, can we ask another favor? There's been some strange critters in the sewers lately. The owner of the biggest casino is searching for talented adventurers! If you're so inclined, seek him out!"

"The biggest casino? …The owner there helped Masato and his friends once before; I swear it was in that file…," Hayato muttered. "Very well. I'll swing by Yomamaburg next."

"Thanks again! Bye!"

Solving one issue opened new paths. Hayato was really living that RPG life. With relish.

Meanwhile…

"Okay, let's get back to work!" the foreman cried. "Part-timers, earn your keep!"

"Sure…"

The part-timers in question were, of course…Masato's party.

The Adventurers Guild had forced them to take up mining.

Masato, Wise, and Medhi were all carrying pickaxes, looking extremely gloomy. Mamako had Altura, the Holy Sword of the Ocean, and Porta her shoulder bag. The two of them looked delighted. The party of five headed down the mineshaft. It was pitch-black inside.

"'Ey, li'l merchant, set up the lights for us, wouldja?"

"Yes! Leave it to me!"

Porta followed the foreman's instructions and began installing glowing gems in the wall sockets. "Oh, you're good!" "Thank you!" Her efforts earned accolades.

The miners headed farther in as the roads lit up before them.

After a while…

"Okay, pretty lass. I'm getting parched! Can we get some water?"

"Oh my. Lass? Me, with a son this big? Gosh… Hyah!"

Mamako gave Altura a little swing, and water appeared in the air. To make it easier to drink, it branched out into several thin hose-like sections. "Wow! That's so convenient!" "Drink up, folks!" Mamako's work impressed the entire crew.

Thirst quenched, the miners headed even farther in…and at last reached the active veins. Ore glittered on the walls like magic itself.

"All right, buckle down! Dig, dig, dig! Part-timers, take it away!"

"We'll do our best…," Masato replied.

"Wait, we're seriously doing this?" said Wise. "Like, is this actually adventurer work?"

"We took the job and came all this way, so we can't back out now," Medhi told her.

Mamako was in charge of water, Porta was doing her Traveling Merchant thing and set up a little shop to sell recovery items, and the other three—were doing hard labor.

Wise in particular was getting surly. She tossed her pickax aside.

"Yo, Wise, you can't just do nothing."

"I'm not! We just need to get the ore out, right? My magic'll blast it out real quick, just you watch. *Spara la magia...*"

The instant Wise began her incantation...

All the ore around began to vibrate, unleashing a mysterious hum.

Wise's magic was sealed.

"Huh?! How?!"

"Heyyy, Sage lassie. We're mining ore used for crafting magic-sealin' items here. Careful."

"You've gotta be kidding me!! This is a joke, right?!"

A joke it was not. Her magic was still sealed.

Horrified, she collapsed to the ground, head in her hands.

"This quest is like my personal hell... I wanna go home..."

"I feel ya there, Wise—but get it together."

"Wise has the mental fortitude of tofu. Watch and learn—I can handle any task with perfect aplomb."

Medhi flashed her patented straight-A, teen beauty smile and swung a pickax at a nearby wall. Her build was built for blunt-force damage!

The tip of her tool cracked the stone wall, striking the ore buried within.

The mystery vibrations expanded.

Medhi's magic was sealed.

"Huh?"

"Heyyy, Cleric lassie. If the ore gets rattled, it releases a magic-sealing effect. Watch yourself."

"*Snort.* I knew you had it in you. Thanks for that, comrade."

"But...this is *your* thing, Wise...! It doesn't happen to me! Ever...!"

Rumble rumble!

"Medhi, relax! …Yikes, she's too far gone."

Dark power was spewing out of her, and she began unleashing a yakuza kick upon the poor wall. *Thud thud thud*—doing far greater damage than she had with the pickax. "She's more powerful than an excavator!" The foreman was impressed.

"Geez, will you two take this seriously? We're on the job." Masato left them to their sulks and tantrums and focused on his own work. One swing at a time, the right degree of strength, mining away. Wise and Medhi were staring intently.

"What, am I doing something wrong?"

"Since when are you so dedicated?" Wise asked.

"Uh, it's not *that* big a deal. I just try and get the job done."

"That's true, but…well, you're usually the first to complain, or resort to a childish outburst. I'd gotten so used to it that seeing you like this is…a little creepy, to be honest. Suspicious, even."

"Creepy how?! And suspicious?! I'm just working hard! Nothing weird about that! What do you even want from me?!"

How rude.

They were both still staring at him in puzzlement. He made a face.

"I guess I get it on some level," he said. "I didn't think I'd end up like this, either. Just…I dunno how to put this, but I feel like…this is how men should be."

"Is it?" Medhi asked.

"My dad's here to test me, right? So I don't want to show him my crappy side. 'Cause I feel like if I do, I'll have failed. So…"

"Dumb kids always gotta showboat in front of their dads, huh?" said Wise.

"You make it sound so bad."

"Meaningless male rivalry exists regardless of family ties."

"Don't spell that out! But…you're also totally on the money, Medhi. And that's why…"

Masato put his back into another pickax swing.

The hard rock wall cracked, and translucent ore peered out from beneath. Transparent as crystal, yet strong enough to soak a blow from his pickax without damage. That was *very* durable.

"Mm? What's this thing?"

He managed to pry it out. The entire object was maybe the size of his fist.

As he stared down at it, Porta raced over, practically beside herself. "M-M-M-Masato! Th-that's a raw diamondddd!!"

""A d-d-d-d-diamond?!""

Wise *and* Medhi—and all the other miners—came running over, unable to believe their eyes. A normal enough reaction. This was a diamond. A *real* diamond!

Except…

"Huh, it is? First time seeing one," Masato said, rolling it around his palm like it was nothing.

Then he tossed it to Mamako—who had her hand on Terra di Madre's hilt.

"Your doing, I assume?" he asked.

"Wh-whatever do you mean?"

She quickly hid the Holy Sword of Earth behind her, but too late. She was caught in the act.

She'd used the special mom skill **A Mother's Indulgence**. Fueled by the desire to reward a child's hard work, it allowed her to physically manifest those feelings.

But she'd gone a bit *too* far, and Masato wasn't even mad. He just smiled at her.

"Everything I said was true. And that means I can get through this without you adding any rewards. I'm glad you've got my back, but this time, I'd prefer you stay out of it. Not because I object to it or anything! I appreciate the gesture."

"I see… Well, okay, then. I shouldn't have meddled."

Mamako took the raw diamond from him, put it on the ground, and tapped it lightly with the tip of her sword. The priceless treasure sank back into the ground.

And a moment later everyone felt like the ground beneath their feet had sunk a bit.

"What was that…?"

"Don't worry. It's nothing. Mommy just asked a bit too much of Mother Earth."

"Yeah? Uh, okay, I guess."

"More importantly, Ma-kun, it's time to showboat your meaningless male rivalry!"

"I'm still against both phrasings, but that *is* the plan."

Masato went back to hacking the wall with his pickax. Working steadily, oblivious to the stares of the nearby miners.

The girls still seemed somewhat disgruntled.

And Mamako both respected his position but felt a little sad about it.

When their shift ended and they left the mine, it was evening.

"Oh dear. We'll have to rush to the store before dinner!"

"Don't see Dad anywhere... Whatever. He's not a kid. Let's head on back."

They said good-bye to the miners and took a transport circle back to Catharn, where things seemed to be finally settling down. Most of the people out walking the streets lived in the city; the bulk of them looked to be housewives out doing their dinnertime shopping.

"Okay, Mom, you'll take care of the shopping. I'll swing by the guild and turn in the quest. How about you guys?"

"I'll go with Mama! I can help carry things!"

"Makes no difference to me... Actually, nah, peak grocery store hours are rough, so maybe I'd better go with Masato...".

"I'll accompany Mamako. I'd like to pick her brain on how we should handle Masato's odd behavior."

"Oh, I want in on that—guess I'm on team shopping after all."

"I don't need to be 'handled.' But suit yourself. See you later."

They all headed out, chattering, and Masato turned toward the Adventurers Guild alone.

When he reached the counter...

"Hey, Masato. You're late!"

Hayato was just accepting a giant satchel of coins from the receptionist. Another pile of cash.

This was annoying, but first things first. Masato had to let the receptionist know that his quest was finish—

"Oh, you're back. Cool. Here." *Toss.*

"You're not even gonna let me get to the counter?! And don't go around throwing money!"

The reward came in a small leather pouch. The coins inside jingled. A fraction of what his father had made.

But it was a big upgrade from the weed-pulling job. Masato glanced over at his father with pride.

Demon Lord Hayato noted his heroic son's stubborn streak and returned a satisfied nod. "I like the look in your eye. An all-new you."

"How would you know? You're always at work."

"I know it seems that way, but Mamako has sent me photos of your sleeping face every night—even back when you were little. I've seen more of you than you think."

"Sheesh, Mom..."

"That aside, you're here on your own."

Hayato glanced around, making sure Mamako wasn't present.

"I've got a proposition for you," he said. "Wanna go somewhere with your dad?"

"Like...where?"

"Yomamaburg. They've got plenty of places to have fun, right?"

"You mean like...the casino?"

"Exactly! From what I hear, parents and children are required to play together."

"True. Going there was Mom's idea. So you mean...?"

Hayato nodded. He put his arm over Masato's shoulders, hefting the bag of mums.

"Here we have a father, a son, and some funds. What more could we want?"

"Hmm. I'm certainly into the idea of casinos, so the offer's tempting. If this wasn't an invitation from a Demon Lord, I'd have agreed already."

"Then what say we call this a casino battle between Daddy Demon Lord and his Hero son? We each start with the money we've earned today. Will you accept a challenge from me, the Demon Lord? Or will you turn tail and run?"

"Well, when you put it like that... But still..."

"What's stopping you?"

"I'd better consult Mom before— Gah?!"

The moment "Mom" left his lips, the Demon Lord's arm tightened around his throat.

"Er, Dad? You're choking me!"

"Listen, Masato. Listen well. Your desire to not worry your mother is admirable... But despite that, you know what I think?"

"Wh-what?"

"I think children *should* worry their parents sometimes. That's what makes being a parent worthwhile! You know the old phrase about teachers only remembering the handfuls?"

"Uh, is that a real thing?"

"It is. So go on and make her worry just a little. You're not yet a grown-up! But neither are you a helpless child who can't do anything without your parents around. Sometimes you need to follow your own heart, regardless of what your mother thinks. As the Hero chosen by the Heavens, stretch your wings and take flight. What do you say?"

"That...makes sense."

"Of course it does! And now that you're on board, a follow-up."

The Demon Lord's arm took a firm grip on Masato's shoulders, pulling him to one side, away from the receptionist and other adventurers.

"Just between you and me," he whispered, "when I completed the extermination quest in Yomamaburg, the client—the casino owner—made me an offer. A very tempting one."

"So that's why you offered to take me there—?"

"No, not just to the casino. The owner has started a new enterprise. A little nightlife, if you will. And he asked if I'd give it a test drive."

"What kind of nightlife are we talking here?"

But Hayato just grinned and raised his pinky. Anyone Japanese knew what that meant—*women*.

"A shop open at night, where women work... Y-you mean—?"

One of *those* shops.

Masato was already blushing.

"Dad...is that even legal...?"

"I'll be honest—in the real world, we wouldn't even be having this conversation. But this is a game—a video game. We're just doing a trial run, broadening your horizons—I'm offering you a little worldly knowledge. They said up front it's all good as long as you're accompanied by a guardian."

"Then, I guess I could...but... No, that's—"

"Masato."

The Demon Lord Hayato's voice was stern. He held out a hand for a shake.

"Are you a man?"

Those words really struck a nerve.

Masato met that gaze head-on. The Demon Lord. His father. A man. And reached out to shake...

But then the ground at their feet began to tremble.

This again?!

"Oh no!"

"What's wrong, Masatooooooooaughhhh?!"

Even as he spoke, the ground shot up, breaking through the floor. The shockwave knocked down the building walls, flinging both of them outside.

What had happened? It was all too clear.

The mom skill A Mother's Fangs had activated, seeking out her son's location and disrupting whatever was happening there.

The father-son duo went rolling across the street outside the guild, and a woman appeared behind them.

"Hee-hee-hee. Dear? Ma-kun?"

That voice made both men let out a soundless scream.

Expressions synchronized, they shuddered...and turned around to find Mamako smiling at them. The girls were behind her, looking lost, but they didn't matter now.

In her right hand, Terra di Madre. In her left hand, Altura. Both Holy Swords held tight.

A wild Mamako appeared. What next?

"Wait, why are in we combat?! ...Uh, you...you see, Mom—!"

"Ma-kun, I could've sworn I heard you discussing going to a casino with your father—and then exploring the nightlife together. Was I imagining that?"

"How good are your ears?!"

No matter how far apart they were, Mamako would never miss her son's voice.

"Wait! Calm down, Mom! We can talk this out! Family discussion!"

"Masato, back down! Leave this one to Dad!"

"A Demon Lord protecting the Hero is not a good look, but go for it!"

Masato beat an emergency retreat! Getting as far away as he could!

But his path was blocked. "Stop." "On your knees." Mamako's words had been all the info Wise and Medhi needed. Their gazes were cold as ice. "Use this cushion!" "Very nice of you to offer, but…" He gently rejected Porta's kind gesture, choosing instead to rest his knees in the dirt.

And watched…

As the Demon Lord Hayato raised his greatsword, ready to lay down his life in combat with Mamako.

"Mamako! First, hear this! This was all discussed well in advance! This is something I wish to do for Masato, as his father!"

"I remember. It's a father's job to teach him about bad things. If he gets involved in them without knowing the risks, he might make a mistake he never recovers from. So the first time should be together. As your father did for you, you'll do for Ma-kun. Isn't that what you told me, dear?"

"Exactly! Bad things are still bad, but there is much to be learned from them! Many things you can only learn there! Valuable experience necessary for surviving in the real world! So let this one pass—please!"

Hayato came at Mamako with a mighty spousal declaration. A powerful blow!

But Mamako withstood it, her swords crossed in an X shape to reject his attack.

"Ma-kun is still too young. He's only fifteen!"

"True, but this is a game world! There's no need to treat him like a child here!"

"A child is a child anywhere."

"To a parent, yes. But in developmental terms, children do not stay children forever! A parent's duty goes beyond protection! Sometimes we must release our embrace, and let them take flight on their own—!"

"No."

"But you must…!"

"No."

Mamako's smiley attacks offered two-negatory multi-denial effectiveness, and Hayato's greatsword was deflected.

Then Mamako sheathed both holy blades…and put one hand on her hip, her index finger raised high. Still smiling.

"Dear."

"Wh-what?"

"Tut, tut."

Not as a mother, but as a wife—the scolding cannon fired.

The effect remained unchanged. Light gathered at her fingertip before unleashing an incredibly hot beam. "Huh?" As the Demon Lord gaped, his body was swallowed up in the light, and he was blown away toward the horizon.

Daddy Demon Lord had become a distant star.

"You get no dinner tonight, dear. Hee-hee."

Scolded with love.

Mamako turned on her heel and stepped over to Masato.

"Ma-kun, we're going back to the inn and having dinner." *Grin.*

"R-right… As you wish…"

He was pulled to his feet, and her arms wrapped around him—a little tighter than usual, perhaps as punishment.

"Er, um…Mom? Is Dad okay? I'm kinda legitimately concerned…"

"I'm sure he'll be fine. Hee-hee."

"Uh, no, I really don't think he is…"

Nobody could survive Mamako's scoldings intact.

Masato's first taste of nightlife dissipated like the morning mist, and the Demon Lord was vanquished…

But Hayato still lived.

He was buried deep in a wall over the plateau outside Catharn, his body literally smoking—but unharmed.

He was a Demon Lord and partner to the most powerful mother alive. And not for nothing.

"Sheesh. Dotes on our son so much, she'll protect him from everything. And this is the result! You never change, Mamako."

Prying himself out of the crater, he easily hopped to the top of the plateau.

The transport point nearby was bathed in moonlight. Surprised by the Demon Lord's approach, fairies lurking in the brushes shot up warning lights, fluttering away. A fantastical sight. Probably pretty annoying for them, though.

Hayato leaned against a stone pillar, gazing down at the capital below.

"The final problem is definitely going to be Mamako... She's gonna give me hell. I may have to exercise a tad more caution," he muttered gloomily.

But then a light descended on the transport point. Someone had arrived.

Shiraaase.

"Oh? I didn't expect to find a Demon Lord here. I imagined you'd be crying into your wife's food again."

"I'm in the doghouse at the moment, I'm afraid. As for my earlier request..."

"Preparations are complete. The stage for the final battle should be ready, somehow, by tomorrow evening."

"And our assistants?"

"Readily accepted. They say tomorrow works for them, but they're already on their way. I'm here to meet and greet. Until further word arrives..."

"Keep up the good work."

Shiraaase vanished into the light once more.

Hayato reached into his pocket and took out a piece of paper.

The fairies around kicked up a fuss.

"Look! The man with the scary sword is reading something!"

"Must be mulling over his plans! Evil plans!"

"I know! Anyone with a sword like that must be a Demon Lord! And they're always up to no good!"

Their hackles raised further, they made themselves scarce.

Hayato grinned at their adorable babble, but his smile soon faded—and he looked at the paper with an expression befitting a Demon Lord.

On it was written a single word: MAMARAID. It depicted a scantily clad woman—an ad for a cabaret.

Whatever other plans he had afoot, this Demon Lord didn't give up easily.

Parent and Child Awareness Survey

Adventurer Final Exam Vol. 2

Are you close to your mother?
I believe our relationship is in tip-top shape.

Do you talk with your mother? How often?
We stick to report, inform, and consult.

Has your mother said anything lately that made you happy?
She said she was proud of me, and that made me ecstatic.

Has your mother said anything lately that made you unhappy?
Something about dark power... I have no idea what she's talking about.

Do you ever go shopping with your mother?
We often did, and I intend to keep that up.

Do you help your mother?
Where I can. I don't want to slow her down.

What does your mother like?
Being the best.

What does your mother hate?
Sloth, filth, poverty, or anything negative.

What are your mother's strong points?
She always has my happiness in mind.

What are your mother's weak points?
Her tendency toward vanity.

If you went on an adventure with your mom, would you become closer?
Not only did we get closer, I believe we've forged a lasting bond.

Answers: Medhi

Chapter 3 Those Who Set Foot in the Forbidden Realms Experience Three Kinds of Hell.

The sun had just barely emerged over the horizon.

Mamako was excitedly moving down the hall of the inn—with stealthy steps—headed for Masato's bedroom.

"I bet Ma-kun's overslept again today. Mommy has to gently wake him! He's such a child. Hee-hee."

Time for a morning kiss on the cheek? Or maybe on the forehead? But as she slowly opened the door to his room...

"Mm? Oh, Mom. Good timing, but remember to knock."

Masato was already up.

And not just up. He'd already changed into his equipment. His pajamas and the blanket were neatly folded on the bed. The window was open, and the room was airing out. He'd taken care of everything.

Mamako looked at all of this, then back at her son. She stood there in shock.

"Come on, Mom. Don't give me that look!"

"B-but...you're up and about...and all on your own..."

"I can manage that much if I feel like it. Nothing cool about relying on you for everything. I figured I could do better."

"You did...?"

"Yep. Ha! How do you like that? Go on, rejoice! Your son is growing up!" He flashed her an impish grin.

And Mamako puffed out her cheeks.

"Wait, why are you sulking?"

"Oh, no reason. Nothing at all. Mommy's just feeling cross."

"What do you have to be mad about here?! That literally makes no sense."

"I'll be cross if I want to be. I'm going to give you extra helpings of everything this morning, Ma-kun! Just you wait!"

"Is that supposed to be a punishment?!"

It was rare to see Mamako this vexed, but he didn't have time to worry about that. Masato had something to talk to her about.

"A-anyway, Mom—I need to ask a favor…"

"Oh my! You want Mommy to do something for you? What is it?" *Flash!*

Every inch of Mamako began to glow. A Mother's Light activated.

"Wow, that sure perked you up fast. I'm so lost… Fine, whatever— my point is…"

He reached into his pocket and pulled out a tie—the gift Mamako had given him for Christmas.

"I wanna put this on, but I dunno how to tie these things. Do you?"

"Your father always wears one to work, so I know the basics—but what brought this on?"

"Well, the receptionist at the guild always looks down on me, right? So today I thought I'd try dressing up. Make a good impression, see where that gets me."

"I see… That makes sense. Leave this to Mommy."

Mamako took the tie from Masato and tied it for him, making it so he just had to pull it over his head and tighten it.

"Ma-kun, could you bend over just a little bit?"

"Okay… Erk…"

That left his face headed right into her valley, but as long as he kept his eyes closed…

She looped the tie over his head.

"Now I just pull the thin end?"

"Let Mommy do it."

She adjusted the fit, straightened his collar, fussing over every detail, taking her time…until it was all perfect.

Masato equipped a tie!

His mature appearance leveled up! Masato obtained the title New Hire!

"Wow, this game tracks some weird levels. Thanks, Mom."

"You're welcome. You can ask Mommy for anything whenever you want, okay? Mommy is always here for you. Forever."

"Don't worry. Soon as I learn how to tie it, I'll be doing it myself. Don't need you doing this forever!"

"Hmph. Ma-kun, Mommy's cross again!"

"That's not something to get mad about! You should want me to grow up!"

"So mad!"

A mother's heart is full of mysteries.

The party finished breakfast and headed to the Adventurers Guild.

Masato took the lead. There was no telling when that receptionist might be watching. The passersby were all potential clients. He had to keep it together, and his gait was as beautiful as it was swift.

The rest of his party was struggling to process this.

"My arms are killing me...," Wise grumbled. "But anyway, something's up with Masato. Porta, appraise him."

"Okay! ...Hnggg...it's definitely the real Masato! He's always cool, but today he's extra cool! He seems so grown-up!"

"Porta, try appraising him more closely. There's clearly something wrong with him. Masato is never this put together."

Medhi's comment was especially rude.

But Masato just laughed it off.

"It's all part of growing up!" he said. "I can't be a kid forever. You guys should follow my example!"

"Ugh, I hate it. You're *Masato*! You're supposed to be incompetent! ...Mamako, please say something. This isn't the son you know!" Wise slapped Masato's back emphatically.

Mamako was trailing along at the back of the party, a deep frown on her face.

"Mamako? What's wrong?"

"......Hmm? Oh, Wise? What is it?"

"That's what *I'm* asking. Something on your mind?"

"Perhaps Mamako is merely worried about Masato. Does he seem off to you, as well?"

"Mama! Is Masato sick?"

"Well..." She gave her son's back a long look, hesitating...then ran to catch up to him. "Ma-kun is always Ma-kun. Mommy's adorable son. Nothing will change that. Right, Ma-kun?"

"Whoa!"

She'd put her arms around him tight. Her large chest squeezed up against him, but Masato was used to that now. It didn't bother him.

"Telling you to stop doing that gets me nowhere, so I won't—but at least try and keep it to a minimum, okay?"

"Oh, I will. The minimum necessary hugging." *Squeeze.*

"That wasn't a request to press against me harder! Also, once we reach the guild, I want us to be all serious business, so try and cooperate."

"Okay, I promise. So until we get there…"

Mamako immediately started walking *very* slowly, and he had to drag her along. The girls stayed behind him, still scowling.

But his mind was made up.

"C'mon! Let's defeat that receptionist!"

"Ma-kun, we can't defeat her. We need to make friends."

The party reached the guild. Inside, they found Demon Lord Hayato by the quest board. Despite Mamako's powerful scolding the day before, he looked happy to see her. A very durable Demon Lord.

"Hero and party, good morning. I trust everyone slept well?"

"We certainly did. I'm relieved to see you alive and unharmed."

"I appreciate your concern. Let us continue the trial—but first…"

Hayato eyed Masato and his necktie curiously. Masato looked mildly sheepish.

"Did you have a change of heart?" Hayato asked.

"Yeah, I guess. Figured I should try and do this right. Laugh if you wanna."

"There's nothing to laugh at. I'm impressed—it really feels like you're trying to do your part for society. I'm proud of you, son. But the color of that tie isn't exactly to my taste…"

"Just so you know, Mom picked it out for me."

"W-well, it's very nice! Beautiful, even! Ha-ha-ha!"

Mamako just smiled back at him. A lovely smile. Definitely a smile.

"S-so allow me to present you with a trial."

Hayato took a posting from the board and handed it to Masato.

It read: INTRODUCE PEOPLE TO THE LOVELY ITEMS OUR COMPANY
IS DISTRIBUTING!

Basically a door-to-door sales job, lugging these "lovely" items from
house to house.

As Masato read it over, Medhi leaned in for a look. "That's definitely
not a job for a combat-class adventurer. Your father is winding you up.
He's saying if you can't even handle a task like this, you aren't worthy
of anything greater."

"Ah-ha. Dick move."

"No, no, not at all. I was suggesting we handle this quest together."

"Together? You mean, just the two of us?"

"That's right. The Demon Lord quest is entering the middle act. You
and I will face off directly on the job."

"Heavens! The Hero vs the Demon Lord! On a sales run?!" Medhi
gave a dramatic shout then stifled a laugh. "That's more like the
Masato I know. What a relief."

"You think this is sad, huh? You would. But work is work. I'm gonna
take my dad on with pride."

"I've never worked in sales, either, so it's uncharted territory for
both of us. Will you accept this quest, Masato? If you *can*."

"I got this. I'll conquer the reception desk and earn the right to challenge the Demon Lord!"

Hayato slapped him on the back, and Masato headed into battle.

The receptionist was leaning back like an empress on her throne,
radiating an aura of authority. "My, my, the boy from yesterday—
Masato, was it? Have you learned nothing? Attempting another job
you are wholly unqualified for? Ah, youth. Tee-hee-hee."

"I'm not the boy I was yesterday. Today I'm here to win."

"We'll see about that. It's up to me whether you've earned the right to
challenge the Demon Lord! ...*Ultimate Art: Receptionist Search!* Hngg!"

The receptionist looked Masato over: hair combed neater than the
day before, expression resolute, and...a well-knotted tie.

She seemed nonplussed.

"Y-you're actually... No, that can't be right. You're at the age where
you think leaving the top button of your dress shirt undone is cool!

But not only is it buttoned, you're wearing a flawlessly coordinated tie! Madness!"

"That's how I roll. Make your call! This round belongs to meeeeee!"

"No—noooooo!!"

Masato waved an arm dramatically, slamming the posting down on the counter!

The receptionist took one look at it—and buried her head in her desk. "Hmph…you win."

"Awesome! I won! Victory is mine!"

"Well done, Masato!"

"You did it, Ma-kun! Mommy knew you could!"

Hayato and Mamako both rushed in and gave Masato a double-sided hug. *Congratulations! Congratulations! Thank you!* Words of praise and gratitude echoed all around!

Also.

"Uh, Masato only won thanks to Mamako's taste in ties. Maybe I shouldn't point that out, though."

"And this posting is just as pathetic as the job we did yesterday. This was hardly even a challenge to begin with."

"Um…the receptionist lady did a great job playing along! I'm glad!"

The girls in the peanut gallery offered their own commentary.

Only Masato and Hayato would be taking this quest. Which meant…

"Welcome! How many?"

"Four. I think a patio table would be lovely."

"Right over here. I'll just fetch your menus."

Mamako and the girls were at a café. Relaxing at a table by the side of the road.

They were in Meema, the site of the World Matriarchal Arts Tournament. There was no active tournament, so they were just here to enjoy drinks and people-watch.

"Are you girls ready? I think I'll just have tea."

"I want a parfait! It looks so good!"

"I'll have the tea and cake set."

"I'm gonna have this pancake set. The tea's gonna go perfect with this show across the street."

All eyes turned to the other side of the street, where...

A middle-aged Traveling Merchant with a large bag on his shoulder was standing with Masato and Hayato, each of whom was carrying another large bag in both hands. They were on the job.

"I'll go first and show you how it's done. Watch and learn."

""Yes, boss! Take it away!""

"Okay, then..."

The Merchant went up the front steps to one house and knocked on the door. "Hello! Pardon the intrusion. I'm here to introduce you to a few lovely ite—"

"We've got plenty. Go away."

The owner of the house barely cracked the door open and immediately shot him down before slamming the door in his face. Harsh treatment, but the Merchant didn't bat an eye.

"That's how we do it! A thick skin is key here. Now go split up all the houses on this street between the two of you."

""Yes, boss!""

The Merchant headed to another district.

New salesman Hero Masato and new salesman Demon Lord Hayato were off!

"It's on, Dad! I'm gonna show you what this hero's got!"

"Prepare to bow before the might of the Demon Lord, son!"

"Which of us will sell the most?"

"Fight!"

Masato took the houses on the right, Hayato the houses on the left. Both were off to a running start.

"I'm gonna win this! I have to!"

Masato ran up to the first door and knocked. "Yes?" A nice old lady! Promising. Masato put on his best smile...

But the old lady struck first!

"Oh, no, thanks. Pardon me."

"Huh? No, wait—!"

She'd taken one look at the bag in his hands, knew he was a door-to-door salesman, and shut that door tight. His pitch failed.

"Argh, fine… Next!" Recovering, he knocked on the door to the right.

He heard someone running up, and the door opened—and was closed again instantly. All he heard was a voice behind it saying, "Go away!" Encounter failed.

"They're rejecting me way too fast… Even metal slimes let you see 'em before they flee…"

This did not seem an impasse he could break through. He was already on the verge of tears.

How was the Demon Lord doing? He turned to check…

"Get the hell outta my face!"

"Bwuh?!"

The old man at the door had flung a bucket of water at him.

The drenched Demon Lord looked over at Masato. Both of them had tears in their eyes.

This job is worse than I imagined! father and son thought alike.

Meanwhile, problems at the café.

"Mama! Calm yourself! You can't go over there!"

"Please, don't stop me! I must be with Ma-kun! He's trying so hard! How can I just watch?! Mommy will buy all the products he's carrying!"

"Not allowed! Get a grip! …Argh, Medhi! Do something!"

"Don't put this on me! I can't exactly beat Mamako down, can I?"

"Fair. Then we'll have to restrain her with brute force!"

The relaxed teatime people-watching had somehow transformed into a desperate scramble to keep Mamako from vaulting over the patio railing, wallet in hand.

Since Meema citizens had proven hostile, the Merchant led Masato and his father to the seaside town of Thermo.

As the tower dungeon loomed above, they began their rounds.

"We didn't sell a thing in Meema, so…I at least want one sale here!"

"New contest, Masato: Let's see who makes a sale first!"

"Yeah! And the contest ends the moment one of us manages it!"

"Naturally!"

Having lowered their hurdle significantly, their motivation was boosted accordingly.

Meanwhile, on the beach...

Someone else was getting really motivated—Mamako, in a swimsuit.

"Wise, Medhi, Porta... Would you mind letting me through?"

Her expression grim, Mamako took a step forward across the hot sand. Her boobs rocked, doing their best to escape her suit.

But the girls, also in swimsuits, couldn't let her go. They desperately tried to block her path.

"No, we can't!" Wise shouted. "Not one step farther!"

"Mamako, snap out of it! Please!" Medhi begged.

"We're just here to play on the beach!" said Porta. "We're not here to buy anything!"

"I only need a moment. I won't be long! I'll just buy one... Ma-kun, I'm coming! Hee-hee-hee..."

"She leaves us no choice!" Medhi yelled. "Bury Mamako in the sand! Everyone—charge!"

""Hahh!""

Between the three of them, they managed to get Mamako onto the ground and started heaping sand on her. "Eep! Her boobs are deflecting all the sand!" "How bouncy can one pair be?! So jealous!" Was it even possible to keep Mamako down?!

Oblivious to the girls' struggles, Masato and Hayato set to work.

"I'll take the houses over here!"

"Then I'll take this side. Forward!"

Both knocked at the same time!

Masato's side opened first. A middle-aged woman!

Oh, I know her...

Definitely one of the moms from Mom's Guild. She'd helped with the tower conquest.

But all her memories of Masato were sealed away. She was looking at him like a total stranger.

"Who might you be?"

"Nice to meet you! Sorry to just drop in. I've got some new items to show you!"

"Oh, you do? A door-to-door sales pitch, hmm? Not really my thing..."

She'd mustered a vague smile and started to close the door. Another bust...?

No! Masato had spotted a change. This was a mother! Masato had adventured with his own mother long enough to know how these creatures operated.

"One moment, please! I've got some slightly unusual accessories to show you!"

"Accessories? Oh my, that is tempting. I suppose I could take a look, at least. Just a peep, mind you."

"Okay!"

Brooches, earrings, necklaces, handbags—anything categorized as an "accessory" would always get their attention. That was a mother's nature! Possibly all women.

Masato quickly got his bag open and pulled out the merchandise and explanatory notes. He was selling little crystal balls.

"Er...what are those?"

"Accessories for your room! Take a closer look, ma'am. These glow just by holding them up! Amazing, right? Like magic! Your children will be delighted. For the foyer, the bedroom, or one of each!"

He was hoping to make a sale, but then—

"Yo, got a sec?"

"Huh...?"

Someone behind Masato called out to him. He turned around to find a mohawk-sporting roustabout scowling ferociously.

Pocchi. Memories sealed—didn't remember Masato at all.

"H-hello! Can I help you?"

"Don't gimme that salesman crap. C'mere."

He grabbed Masato by the scruff of his neck and dragged him away.

The street was now filled with rough-looking men—and another one was manhandling the Demon Lord, who looked just as crestfallen as his son.

They soon found themselves kneeling on the ground, surrounded by burly young roustabouts.

"Lemme make the introductions. We're a bunch of nice guys hoping to become daycare workers. We protect this here town and all the children in it."

"I have no idea what daycare has to do with this..."

"Dad, just hear him out. It's a hundred percent true. Shocking, I know."

"So there we were, on patrol, and we find you punks. Selling *crystals*. Bullshit artists!"

"What is your issue with our approach?" Hayato inquired.

"Not long ago there was a big mess here. A creepy salesman sold everyone crystals that turned out to be bombs!"

"That was you, though, Pocchi."

"Wha—?! Don't bullshit a bullshitter, man! I'd never do that!"

He'd yelled his way out of this one.

"So we're gonna take you two over to the guard station! On your feet!"

"Don't treat us like criminals... We're innocent, I swearrrr..."

Work was interrupted for an interrogation.

The perils of the modern workplace.

In a fragrant room with mood lighting, Mamako let out a rapturous breath.

"Mm...no, not there...ahh..."

She was sprawled on a bed without a stitch on her as six hands assailed her body.

The instant they touched her sensitive spots, her back arched and her ample bosom, covered in sticky fluid, heaved.

No matter how she protested, the hands wouldn't stop.

"You like it here? Heh-heh-heh. Then... Hyah!"

"Eep!"

"How about here?"

"Aah!"

"Mama! How's this?"

"Nooo...!"

Wise, Medhi, and Porta's hands were all slick with oil, assaulting Mamako.

An oil massage.

"You're all so good! I'm making the oddest noises."

"Thanks," said Wise. "I knew your shoulders had to be stiff. I mean, hauling those two weights around all the time, who wouldn't be super sore? …I'd like to blame a bad back on my boobs once in my life…"

"Some dreams are better left unfulfilled. It's legitimately painful."

"Tch, Medhiii! We know you're second only to Mamako! Don't rub it in."

"Mama's calves are also stiff! She spends a lot of time on her feet cooking and doing laundry!"

"I can only imagine," said Medhi. "That's why we're giving her a full-body massage. Hyah!"

"Ohhhh!"

This was all designed to keep Mamako in place.

They were in a room somewhere in Yomamaburg. A beauty salon with large windows and a commanding view, and they had the whole place to themselves. The girls were giving Mamako the best pampering they could.

"Is this the spot, Mamako? Do you like that?" Wise asked.

"Y-yes! Perfect…ahh!"

"Heh-heh-heh. Your body doesn't lie! Is that what we say here?"

After a particularly vigorous tour of Mamako's nether regions, Wise took a break. Her hands were tired.

And as part of that, she opened the curtains, looking down at the city below—where Masato was going door-to-door.

He and Hayato had abandoned Thermo and resumed their father-son competition…but without results. The sun was about to set.

But Masato would not give up.

"…Geez, what is he doing? Talk about a pointless struggle—so dumb."

"Indeed. No regard for us at all, totally obsessed with the task at hand."

Medhi had sidled up beside Wise and was also watching Masato.

There was a sad edge to their grumbling.

"He's been like this since his dad showed up. All this father-son brouhaha… You'd think they could spare us a little attention."

"You miss him already, Wise?"

"That's *not* what I said!"

"I miss him! It's like Masato's going further and further away, and we're being left behind." Porta had joined the two of them at the window.

"Yes! I know just how you feel, Porta."

And there was Mamako. "Mamako, you can't be here!" "They can see you from outside!" "Oh, that's not a problem." "I think it is!" The three of them had to physically block Mamako's nude form from view.

Mamako looked over their heads at Masato's toils. "...Ma-kun...," she whispered.

He never knew. How could he? They were far apart. And her voice was very soft. A sad smile played across her lips, and she moved back to the bed, lying facedown.

"Mamako...?"

"I suppose...there's nothing odd about it. Children grow up. They find things they want to do, things they *have* to do, and get absorbed in them...and we grow apart. That's normal. A part of life. How things are meant to be. But..."

She still missed him.

She left that unsaid, keeping her head down to hide her gloomy expression.

And in that instant...

""""......?"""""

A strange sensation swept over the three girls.

It was similar to how a blow to the knees can make your legs fold under you. Like their gazes had dropped several inches in a single moment—very odd.

Perhaps they'd just imagined it. Mamako didn't react at all. Nothing in the room or out the window seemed different.

"Did something weird just happen?"

"I don't know! But I felt kinda spinny!"

"Yeah, same here... Weird. Like, a sudden dizzy spell maybe?"

"Now that you mention it...perhaps that explains it."

They left it at that and turned back to look out the window, where Masato was still hard at work.

"…I guess I just want him to mess up bad. Do something that lets us punish him."

"I agree with you. That would be an excellent way to lift our moods."

"I'd certainly like to see him be more like himself! …Um, not that I think messing up is…what Masato does, or anything…"

"Hee-hee. Maybe I should get in on that! I would feel much better if he did something that reminded us he's still my Ma-kun."

Not what Masato would have wanted to hear—and as they spoke, he sneezed. Perhaps the old wives' tale was true: Sneezing means someone's gossiping about you. The girls looked at each other and laughed.

All four of them. "Argh, Mamako!" "Contain yourself!" "They'll see you!" "Oh my. Such a shame." You couldn't let your guard down with her around.

The sun had set, and work was done.

"Both the boy and girl teams survived the day," said Wise.

"Time for the results of the Hero vs Demon Lord contest," said Medhi.

"Um… About those results…," Porta began.

The girls were looking said results in the face: Masato and Hayato, on a bench together, shoulders slumped.

"Neither of us sold a single thing…"

"And these unfortunate results mean our contest is a draw…"

"Draws suck…"

They were getting gloomier by the minute. Downright dismal.

Mamako was patting both their backs. "You two worked hard! But however tough it was, the workday is finished. It's time to relax."

"…True," said Masato. "Work's done. It's all over."

"Yes. The end of the workday is cause for celebration," agreed Hayato.

Mamako's praise comforted the two injured souls. Father and son lifted their heads and stretched.

"Let's head back to Catharn," Mamako said. "I need to get dinner started."

"Time to fire up a transport spell! …Medhi, duel you for it?"

"You're on."

A quick round of rock, paper, scissors—Medhi won. Wise scowled but started the incantation nonetheless.

But then…

"Wait just a minute."

Demon Lord Hayato interrupted her.

"Masato and I have further business to take care of. We'll be staying behind."

"Huh? Wait, Dad, what business…? There's more?!"

"There is. Our labor is over, but our task is not yet done."

"Ugh…" Masato buried his face in his hands.

Pretending to comfort him, careful not to let anyone see, the Demon Lord held out a hand—like he was going for a shake.

And there was a flyer folded up in his palm. Masato could just make out the word *cabaret*.

A-again…?

"*Are you a man?*"

The look in Hayato's eyes said it all. He'd not yet lost this battle.

Masato…returned his father's handshake, that same look in *his* eyes.

"Well, if the task needs completing…" *Smile.*

"Ladies, you all head back first. We may be rather late, so feel free to eat without us." *Smile.*

"Hmm… All right, then…" Convinced, Wise started her chant again. Father and son saw her off with a smile…

"Hee-hee. Dear? Ma-kun?"

""Erk…""

Mamako's smile, meanwhile, just proved she was deeply *un*convinced.

"What task might this be, dear?"

"W-w-well, clearly, work stuff! Post-work bonding! Extremely necessary. We all do it!"

"That's true, but…Ma-kun's hungry. You want to fill your belly up with Mommy's cooking, don't you?"

"I mean, yeah, that *is* always tempting! But this is work stuff. That Merchant guy asked us to join him, and we can't well refuse…right, Dad? That's what this is!"

"Exactly! Masato is absolutely correct. That Merchant seems to like us! He was kind enough to invite us out, and he's been a great help, so it would be rude to turn him down! Don't you agree, Mamako?"

"In principle, yes. Hmm..."

Mamako wavered. An opening! *Go!!* Masato and Hayato made eye contact and took their best shot!

Together, they each put their arms around Mamako!

Father-Son Coaxing! A special father-son skill that worked only on mothers!

"Please, Mom. Just this once!"

"Please, Mamako. Just this once!"

"Oh my... Argh. You're both incorrigible. I suppose I could make an exception."

""Thank you! We love you!""

Cuddling made her so happy, it corrupted her judgment... This skill hit mothers where it hurt. They successfully made Mamako back down.

"Well, Masato. Let's go be incorrigible!"

"Absolutely! Let's see how incorrigible we can be!"

Dreamily, Mamako watched them go. The girls mostly seemed appalled; the boys were gone before anyone could change their minds.

Shoulder-to-shoulder, Hayato and Masato headed to the Yomamaburg entertainment quarter. Row after row of casinos, lights so bright they seemed liable to add color to the darkness of the night sky.

The streets were packed. Since the rules required parents and children to play together, there were plenty of older folks walking side-by-side with younger men and women.

Masato and Hayato walked together with pride, as father and son.

But then Masato paused.

"Something wrong, son? Not losing your nerve already, are you?"

"That's not it. I was just wondering if we're making a terrible mistake. There's tons of issues with me being here—and the same goes for you, Dad."

"Such as, a married man shouldn't be doing this?"

"Pretty much."

Masato gave him a searching look, but the Demon Lord didn't bat an eye.

"Masato, I need you to listen to me. That argument is irrelevant. We're just out for a good time. It's all in good fun. This is one way that men enjoy themselves. In other words, it has nothing to do with love."

"It doesn't?"

"Not a thing. Completely unrelated."

Hayato was very insistent, but this logic was pretty patriarchal.

"But if you still find yourself feeling guilty, then make it up to the one you love. Give her presents, help her with her work, get on her good side. That sort of attention is very important."

"I see. This is highly educational."

"Masato, later on, you just have to do right by Wise or Medhi. Or even Porta!"

"Wai— Why are we talking about them? They're not part of this!"

"Just a little payback. Your fault for reminding me of my wife."

"F-fair. Sorry. Shouldn't have brought it up. I won't do it again."

"Good. Let's get going!"

The Demon Lord pulled out the cabaret flyer, checking the map. Then he headed down a narrow alley between two casinos, Masato on his heels.

The farther they went, the more the bustle died down. The lights faded. The dubiousness went way up.

The only sound was their own footsteps, headed down the dark alley… until they found a sign standing in their path reading MAMARAID. A very discreet exterior.

An elderly gentleman in a perfectly tailored suit stood outside, smiling warmly. It was the casino owner who had once helped Masato's party out.

"But his memories are sealed, so he doesn't remember me."

"We chatted briefly while I was working with him yesterday, but no, he didn't remember you. So leave this to me! …Good evening, owner. Sorry it took me so long."

"Not at all! I quite understand. I was aware the request was fraught with difficulties." He bowed to Masato, too. Unfailingly polite to everyone. "Now, allow me to get your nightlife trial experience started. Do come in. I changed jobs from God of Gamblers to God of the Entertainment District, and I'm confident you'll enjoy the fruit of my labors."

The doors to adulthood swung open...!

The interior was a dramatic departure from the drab exterior—everything was so gaudy, it was almost sickening.

Right inside they were met with the dazzle of a chandelier. The walls gleamed with gold. The floor was black and shiny.

And on it stood a row of beautiful women in ravishing evening gowns. Humans, elves, beastkin, angels, and devils, too. A cross-species cabaret lady buffet.

""""""Welcome!""""""

""G-glad to be here...""

Every single lady smiled at both father and son, who bowed their heads in greeting.

Masato was quickly blushing—and so was Hayato. They looked nervous.

"Why are *you* stressing this, Dad?"

"Why wouldn't I? I've never been anywhere like this! ...Frankly, I'm not at all clear how these shops work."

"Wait—you can't drop a truth like that here! What the heck are we supposed to do?! I have no clue how this works, either!"

"No cause for alarm," said the owner. "This establishment is set up to ensure the safety of our customers. It employs the same system as the casinos do. Anyone can enjoy the services here free of worry." The owner clapped his hands and directed the pair's attention to the girls. "Ladies, these customers are new to the cabaret experience. Take care to guide them through it. Make sure there are no awkward moments. You were all once the top earners at shops the world over, so I'm sure you're up to the task."

""""""We are, owner!""""""

"Pleased to hear it. Gentlemen, do enjoy."

The owner left, and the girls gathered round Masato and Hayato.

A beautiful girl in every direction. Very close. Lots of skin. They all smelled amazing. Hands reaching out and taking his. Arms around his. Things pressing against him!

"I think I'll sit with this dandy gentleman."

"O-oh? Well, be gentle…"

"Then I'll take this young charmer. Come! Two to the floor!"

"Th-thanks…"

"Where shall we sit? Open seating? No—a private room."

"Naturally. They're the owner's guests! They get the red carpet treatment."

"The harem course it is!"

""""""Thanks for coming!"""""

"D-Dad! This sounds like a whole thing! Are we still okay?"

"I dunno! But let's go with 'yes'! Have some faith!"

Both men had a knockout on each arm, plus more girls in front and behind. It was less "guide" and more "apprehend."

The central section of the shop was a large open area. At the back were two doors—judging from the decor, very expensive ones. These must be the private rooms.

"Here we are. First, dandy gentleman, take the room on the right."

"Er, wait, we're in separate rooms?"

"That's how the harem course works. Come on!"

"No, wait! Dad, don't!"

He tried to stop it, but Masato was surrounded by cabaret girls and unable to move. He lacked the nerve to push a pretty lady out of the way.

Demon Lord Hayato looked extremely perturbed. "Godspeed, Masato!" he said, and the doors to his room slammed shut.

"Handsome son, yours is the room on the left. This way."

"Urp… Uh, look…I dunno if I'm ready… I-I'd better go home! This doesn't feel right for me!"

"Oh my. First time? In that case, we could set you up with one of our new girls. They might not be up to *our* standards, but sometimes, that helps you relax."

"That's not the problem—!"

"We'll go get them. You wait in here."

Masato was pushed into the private room. His escort blew him a kiss, and the doors closed.

These doors were bad news—they could be opened only from the outside.

It wasn't exactly spacious, but the circular couch was clearly higher quality than the ones on the open floor.

There was a coffee table in the center with tumblers, champagne flutes, and other pricey-looking glasses. And a pitcher of water.

Clearly, the idea was to fill these with booze and sip away as you chatted with your female companions. Masato could imagine that much.

"...Yikes."

He was really here.

Masato gingerly settled down on the couch facing the entrance. He wasn't sure how to greet whoever came in, and got nervous about it, so he slid along the couch until his back was to the door.

Then he just waited.

"...I've gotta make it clear that I'm leaving. Just...gotta tell them. Yeah. I'm a man! I can speak my mind!"

He muttered this on a loop, like he was trying to conjure evil spirits.

Then there was a knock at the door. They were here!

Masato was a man! A very determined man! "...C-come in," he said, his voice thin and reedy. He couldn't decide what look he should have on his face and settled for staring at his hands. Already defeated.

The door behind him opened, and someone came in. By the footsteps...one, two, three...four.

They were being very quiet. No one said a word.

They said these girls were new...so maybe they're also nervous...?

Masato was so anxious, he was about to die. Then someone flopped down on his right. Someone else took a seat on his left—in a much more dignified manner.

Two more took seats across from him. Four ladies in total.

Nobody spoke. They'd brought a bottle in a bucket of ice with them and set that on the table—he could hear the clink of ice settling.

Am I gonna have to speak first? Wh-what do I say?

He couldn't take the silence any longer. Slowly, he forced his eyes up.

81

Legs came into view—women's legs. The four ladies around him were each wearing a different-colored evening gown.

As he eyed their legs, the woman on his right suddenly stood. She got up, sidled close to him, then sat down again, arm around his shoulders. She whispered in his ear:

"What the hell are you doing here? Maybe I oughta rat you out to Mamako."

"No, please, have mercy— Wait."

He knew that voice. His head snapped up.

Wise's mom, the Queen of the Night—Kazuno.

"...Buh?"

"'Sup. How you been?"

Definitely Kazuno. And not just her.

Across from him on the right: Shiraaase. On the left: Porta's mom, Dark-Mom Deathmother.

And on his left was Medhi's mom, giving him her gnarliest glare: Medhimama.

"Huh?! Wait—what's going on here—?!"

"That's what we want to know, Masato. Why are *you* in a shop like this? You'd better have a good excuse."

"Simmer down, Memama. That can wait. First, drinks and cheers. Gotta have a few in a shop like this! I've spent plenty of time in host clubs, so trust me on this one."

"Kazuno! What is wrong with you? Explanations come first!"

"Head's up, Medhimama!" Shiraaase said, intentionally aiming the champagne cork at her.

"W-wait—" *Pop.* "Ow!" It hit Medhimama smack in the forehead. She wailed, clutching her brow. Ideal.

"Nice one, Shriaaase. Hey, Saorideath, gimme a glass. I'm thirsty."

"Could we refrain from the odd names, please? Oh, why do I bother?" said Deathmother. "Masato, yours is nonalcoholic, of course. We'd heard you were underage and came prepared."

"Oh, cool."

Champagne and a champagne-like soda were poured and passed around.

"Then let's drink to our reunion! Cheers!"

""""Cheers!""""

Glasses clinked, and everyone took a sip. The bubbles felt great going down.

Kazuno chugged hers and pressed herself up against Masato.

"Whoa, Ms. Kazuno?! Don't do that!"

"Heh-heh, why not? This is a cabaret, and I'm a cabaret girl! This is all part of the job."

"Yeah, but—!"

"Don't worry. Enjoy the perks. How's it feel to have a friend's mom waiting on you?"

"Unspeakably awkward," came Masato's despondent reply.

"Pshaw. You know you love it. So? Why are you here?"

"Right! Explain yourself! You should not be in a shop like this at your age!" Medhimama had recovered from the cork to the head. She grabbed a fistful of Masato's shirt, scowling like a thing possessed, and began shaking him. His brain hurt.

"C-calm down! I'll explain! It's basically for a work thing…that my dad brought me to! The whole idea was that you're with your parent, so it's safe to do a trial experience."

"Some things are still off limits, parent or no! I can't believe this. I won't stand for it! Not at all! This should not be! Where is your father now? I'm gonna give him a piece of my mind. I might even— *Gasp, cough.*"

"Honestly, you shouldn't talk that long without breathing. Memama, drink up."

"Oh, how thoughtful, Kazuno. Don't mind if I do!"

Medhimama chugged her champagne, wetting her throat, and turned to fire her machine guns at Masato again…

"*Hic.*"

Her face was red. Her eyes bleary. She cuddled up against him.

"Yikes?!"

"Masatooo! Hear me out… *Hic*… I'm suuuch a mess… *Hic.*"

Medhimama was instantly plastered. From one glass. "Heh-heh-heh." Kazuno was definitely doing the Queen of the Night laugh. Clearly well aware Medhimama couldn't hold her liquor. Diabolical.

"Masato, are you even listening? You *gotta* listen, or else I'm gonna bite your ear off! Maybe I will anyway!"

"O-okay, I'm listening! Listening hard! What is it?"

"It was awful! The whole thing—a total con! Only way to pay it back is this job... *Hic*... I can't taaake it!"

"I'm so lost."

"Allow me to interpret."

"I can infooorm—as I am Shiraaase."

Dark-Mom Deathmother and Shriaaase moved around behind Masato, resting their boobs on his shoulders.

"Wait, are you both drunk, too?"

"Oh, you sit still. Don't fuss, just listen," said Deathmother. "Your father asked us to come over—help with the Demon Lord quest, he said. But we arrived at the meeting spot ahead of schedule..."

"And decided to kill some time seeing the sights," Shiraaase continued. "We wound up gambling in the biggest casino here..."

"Oh, I get it. You lost big, racked up a debt, and have to work it off here? Right?"

"Exactly. I got roped into it, too."

"I can infooorm you that Kazuno and Medhimama did the deed, and Deathmother merely got dragged along. Just like their daughters always do."

"Like mother, like daughter. Got it. Then..."

With the explanation over, he thought they'd go back to their seats. But Dark-Mom Deathmother and Shiraaase remained in place, leaning into him closer and closer. Very intimate.

"...Um, ladies?"

"Perhaps I'm drunk, too. I'm starting to enjoy this. You've always been there for Porta, so these are for you, on the house. Hee-hee."

"I merely want to tease you, Masato. But, well...perhaps this once, I should be serious. I may be the mother of a five-year-old, but I still know a few moves. Hee-hee-hee."

"Not so fast, Shiraaase. I'm gonna take young Masato for myself. So, Masato—it's time you fooled around with a friend's mom. Mwa-ha-ha-ha-ha."

"Ugh, Masatooo! You're not *listening*! I'm gonna bite your ear off!"

Kazuno and Medhimama were both squeezing harder.

Masato was getting mobbed by the affections of four mothers at once. For a game played by mothers and children together, he'd managed the impossible—an all-mom harem!

Masato was beside himself…!

Yeah. I really wish they wouldn't.

Okay, maybe not exactly "beside himself."

Best to change the subject. He happened to have a specific concern.

"Q-question for you! A serious one, so if you don't mind infooorming me?"

"That calls for me, Shiraaase! How may I be of assistance?" *Ding!*

"How is it even possible to run up a debt in the casino? This town's got a special rule in place to prevent that. If children are going wild, it automatically drags in their parents. And if the parents are too far in, it brings in the kids…"

"This is true, but I can infooorm you we took the system offline temporarily to allow everyone to thoroughly enjoy themselves."

"Ah, right."

The conversation ended there. Back to moms all over Masato. The mom harem antics weren't finished yet—

But wait.

"……Hmm?"

He remembered something.

"This establishment is set up to ensure the safety of our customers. It employs the same system as the casinos do. Anyone can enjoy the services here free of worry."

The owner's words.

"…Huh?"

Masato was covered in moms gone wild. Shiraaase's daughter wasn't playing this game, but the other three definitely had kids in-game.

Which meant…

"……Uh, I'm in trouble."

The blood drained from his face.

Just then, there was a soft knock at the door.

"…Come in," he said.

In came four girls dressed in full cabaret attire, with the loveliest smiles to match. Mamako, Wise, Medhi, and Porta.

Shiraaase remained unflappable no matter the occasion, but Masato, Kazuno, drunk Medhimama, and Dark-Mom Deathmother all froze on the spot, looking like disaster had befallen them.

The girls' smiling faces bore down upon Masato.

The frozen group couldn't move, let alone run.

"I guess they weren't kidding about 'mama raid'... Ah, such a short life..."

Masato abandoned hope and closed his eyes to the inevitable.

Thus...

"It seems this is as far as we go."

Demon Lord Hayato's voice echoed from somewhere. A magic circle appeared beneath Masato and his mom harem.

The girls' smiles vanished. Everyone looked tense.

"Oh my? What's this?"

"That's the same pattern as the transport spells!" Porta yelled. "This is bad!"

"Masato's dad is trying to let our moms escape!" said Wise. "Over my dead body! We've gotta stop this!"

Wise threw herself at Kazuno, but a moment too late. Kazuno vanished in a flash of light. "Bwah?!" And Wise landed face-first on the couch. Looked pretty painful.

"Damn it, Masato's dad! What was that for?!"

"My apologies. I have need of your mothers elsewhere; I can't have them taken away just yet. I'm afraid we must be off."

"Yeah, right! No way *my* mom would ever be useful! I'm about to give her a piece of my mind! Bring her back!"

"And while Wise's screeching has him distracted... Mother!"

Medhi had been sneaking up on her mother, but... "Augh...!" Just as her hands made a grab for her collar, Medhimama was teleported elsewhere.

"Oh no! My mommy's gonna be taken away, too! Mommyyy!"

"Ah, my beloved daughter! You still call me that, despite my utter foolishness!"

Porta tried to leap into Dark-Mom Deathmother's arms, to her mother's evident delight. But before they could touch, Deathmother vanished!

Two left.

"Ms. Shiraaase, you're not going anywhere. That's not your role. You're here to infooorm us of the situation, yes?"

"Mamako, if you say that, I would be only too happy to infooorm… Whoops, unexpected twist."

Shiraaase picked up the champagne bottle and bonked herself on the head with it. Shiraaase died, and her coffin was teleported away without another word.

The four mothers had successfully fled. Leaving behind…

"Okay, okay! Nice work, Dad! I'm next, right? Take me away!"

Masato was all for escaping certain doom with a last-minute transport. He could see himself soaring away and was already flapping his arms in anticipation. Any second now…!

The magic circle vanished.

"……Wha?"

No more magic circle. No transport spell. No escape for him.

And the girls' hands were already clenching his clothing. He was caught.

"Dad! What the hell?!"

"Masato, nice work resisting temptation. I've witnessed your growth firsthand—I feel within you the power to progress to the future. And as your father, I've accomplished all I wanted… Thus, it is time for the trial to proceed to the final phase."

"We can talk trial stuff later! Get me outta here first!"

"Son, allow me to leave you a gift."

A tiny magic circle appeared above Masato's head, and a single blue feather fluttered down. As he gaped up at it, it landed on his face.

"That is the key to reaching my location—the ideal spot for a Demon Lord Dad to battle his Hero son… I'll be waiting."

"Yo! This is bullshit! You've gotta get me outta here! Daaaad! Help!"

Demon Lord Hayato's voice was gone.

What now?

Masato's hand closed around the feather, his expression as grim as it was determined.

"Guys, you heard the man! It's time for our final battle! Let us put aside any worldly concerns and steel ourselves for—!"

"Ma-kun, we're going back to our inn in Catharn for a nice little chat." *Smile.*

"...Okay......"

His last-ditch effort to talk his way out of it had failed.

Feeling like a criminal headed to prison, Masato dragged his feet back to the inn. There, he was forced to make a full confession and was handed his sentence.

"Ma-kun, if you regret your choices, then make an offering to those you love."

"I'm fine with cash, personally," said Wise.

"But with your finances, it would be difficult to prepare enough gifts to satisfy us all," Medhi explained, "so physical labor is the only viable alternative."

"I'm not actually that mad, but I want to be like everyone else! Please do this for us!"

In the end, the girls lined up in the bath, and he was told to wash their backs.

The Hero's party was known for its naked strategy sessions, so this time they were doing a naked atonement.

"I'll get right to scrubbing..."

Masato bowed his head low to the row of backs and then lathered up a sponge.

Mamako first. Perhaps because of the oil massage, her back felt extra smooth today. He gently scrubbed away.

"Mom—no, Mother. I apologize deeply for causing you undue concern."

"Oh my! How polite! I know at your age you're curious about these things, but you have to remember how young you still are."

"Yes...I'll take a good hard look at myself and never make a mistake like that again."

"Good. Then the matter's settled…but if I'm being totally honest, I'd like to thank *you*. I feel much more secure now. Hee-hee-hee."

"?"

He wasn't sure what that meant, but he poured a bucket of warm water over his mother, making sure to get the suds out of her intergluteal cleft. One down.

Next was Wise.

"Ultimate Sage Wise. I apologi—"

"Spare me. Just get this over with… Besides, I'm not really that mad. Actually, I'm kinda into this."

"Into it how?"

"That'd be telling. Go on, wash."

"S-sure…"

Wise was laughing, and her shoulders were shaking. He quickly scrubbed her down and poured water over her, watching the beads form on her back. Youth sure made her skin gleam.

Next was Medhi.

"Beautiful Medhi, heart as white as snow. Beg pardon."

"That strikes me as spiteful somehow, but I'll overlook it. I took immense pleasure from today's proceedings."

"Again, why? What does that even mean?"

"Not telling. You might get more out of nice little Porta than a mean girl like me."

"Hoo boy…"

Her hair usually hid the lovely nape of her neck, but now it and her back were on display. He ran a soapy sponge over it, rinsed, and was done.

Last, Porta's little back.

"Princess Porta, healer of my heart and soul. Please, enlighten this poor fool. Why have my failings proved comforting or pleasing?"

"Because they were just what we'd hoped you'd do!"

"Oh?"

"Since your daddy got here, you've been all serious and mature, like a grown-up! Nothing like the old Masato! So—!"

"So when I screwed up again, you were all like, 'Whew!'"

"Yes!"

"Ha-ha-ha. That certainly clears that up. Rahhh!"

He tickled her sides through the suds and she bent backward, giggling. "Eep, it's slipping!" He quickly caught the shoulder bag, balanced it on her head, and the day was saved.

He rinsed Porta's back, giving the other girls a highly disgruntled scowl. They were washing the rest of themselves, humming happily away.

"Well, I wasn't trying to worry anybody. But...sorry, I guess."

"Hee-hee. Apology accepted."

"Hrmph..."

Masato had plenty to grumble about, but was also well aware he deserved a lot more anger here. Best to call it a tie. His reparations were now complete.

He filled a bucket with cold water, put his hands together, and stuck them in. *Squirt, squirt.* ""Wahhh?!"" Shots of very cold water hit Wise and Medhi in the back, and he slipped into the bath itself.

The main bath was quite deep, and he was immediately submerged to his shoulders. The hot water eased the tension of the day's labor.

"Whew...that's the stuff. Ahhh, paradise!"

"What the hell was that for, Masato?!"

"Perhaps you *should* be punished."

Done washing up, Wise and Medhi both jumped into the bath, one on either side of him. They began twisting his arms and legs mercilessly. It hurt. Quite a bit.

Mamako and Porta followed and for some reason joined in on the punishment. For a few minutes, all was bedlam...

But then it fell quiet. Masato had stopped squawking.

He leaned back in the water, staring at the ceiling. Eyes unfocused.

The girls all looked baffled.

"Ma-kun, is something wrong?"

"Maybe."

He held up a hand. In it was the feather the Demon Lord had given him.

An invitation to the final fight. His eyes narrowed.

"...Mom, you and me are pretty close now, right?"

"Yes. A happy family. Mom's seal of approval!"

"You got the Sage's seal, too. No doubts."

"You're so close, no one could possibly argue the point."

"I agree!"

"So we've actually met the conditions to beat the game."

"Oh…" Mamako blinked, her smile stiffening. The others got very quiet.

Eyes locked on the feather, Masato continued. "I've been all about enjoying our adventures here in this game. But then Dad shows up talking about the power to progress to the future, and work…and I got to thinking maybe it's time I started planning for what comes next. Maybe that's Dad's goal here, you know?"

"O-or…maybe the Hero has fallen right into the Demon Lord's cunning trap. Better be careful, Ma-kun—"

"Still," he said, turning his gaze toward his mother. He smiled. "That wouldn't be so bad. Call this battle with Dad the ending, beat the game, and head into the future. The next battle will be in the real world… At least, that's basically what I've been thinking anyway. What's your take on it, Mom?"

"M-Mommy…i-isn't sure. I'll…have to sleep on it…"

It was rare to see her without any answer. Or avoiding his eye.

"Geez. Just when I think you're back to your old self, now you're being all serious again."

"Will you never learn? What business do you have making us this uncomfortable?"

Wise and Medhi each slapped him hard on the back. They were smiling.

"Fine, then! Do it your way, Masato. The Ultimate Sage has your back."

"As do I. On one condition…"

"Namely?"

"Even if we beat the game and dissolve the party, our bonds remain. That much is mandatory."

"And don't go being all grown up on your own. That's *my* condition! You leave us outta this stuff, there'll be hell to pay."

"Why not be bold, Wise? Just say you want to go out with him."

"Huh?! Wai—Medhi?! Where'd that come—"

"I plan to swipe him right out from under your nose." *Grin.*

"Why would I want in on your nasty melodrama?! …B-besides, that kinda thing just happens when it happens… Either way, you cool with those terms, Masato?"

"Sure."

He raised a fist to strike a vow, and both girls bumped it. Promises made…

And both of them quickly put their hands together, squirting hot water in his face. "Argh!" "Ha-ha!" "Payback." Still, a promise was a promise.

Everyone splashed water around for a minute, but then Porta came up to him, looking nervous. "Um, Masato! And Wise and Medhi, too—can I say something?"

"Mm? What's up, Porta?"

"If we go back to the real world, I'll still be in elementary school. Will you still play with me then? I'd really like to hang out or go places together!"

She looked so worried; Masato and the other girls were quick to nod their assent.

"Of course, Porta. You're one of us. Hope you're ready for lots of tickles!"

"Ummm, Masato, that sounds like a criminal charge waiting to happen."

"You can't just play. You've got to study, too. Masato and Wise would make useless teachers, so I'll handle that aspect for you, Porta."

"Wish I could disagree, but yeah…Medhi's the right girl for that job. I'm more the makeup and cooking type. Definitely don't want Medhi doing any cooking."

"Then I'll be like your big brother! …How's that sound, Porta?"

"Great! I feel much better. I'm not worried anymore! I'll help you out, too, Masato!"

"Thanks. Then let us exchange the vow of splashing!"

Everyone readied their hands. "Whoa! I-I can do that, too!" Porta tried to fire, but it didn't go very far. She quickly changed tactics to shoving water with both hands.

As drops of water flew and voices yelped, the bathwater churned...
but it wasn't long before they all stopped.

Someone else should have slipped into the fray, getting closer to
Masato than anyone—but not this time. Mamako still had her head
down, lost in thought.

Mom...

Their adventures had made him better at reading her moods. He
knew exactly what was on her mind.

Beating the game meant the end of their adventure together.

Their time here, adventuring with her beloved son—how thrilling
had that been for her? Everyone knew.

And he'd just suggested they put an end to that joy.

But...it wouldn't be right to take it back.

He was trying to move forward of his own free will. To live his life.
No one had a right to stop that; not even his parents.

But it hurt to put it like that. He didn't want to push his mother
away. He knew it would be best if she could come to terms with it,
so they could move forward together... He hoped Mamako would
understand.

Masato stared at her until she finally looked up.

"...Ma-kun, can we talk?"

"Mm? Sure, Mom."

She reached out her arms, beckoning him. Gesturing for a hug.

"Uh, here? Can we at least get dressed first...?"

"Kinda late to draw that line."

"This is a job for the Hero Son. Have courage."

"Masato! Go ahead!"

"Uh...okay. Fine."

They didn't seem to be mocking him—it was more like deep
understanding.

He gave Mamako a solid hug.

Her breast felt warm against his cheek. And she could feel her son's
warmth, too. She savored the embrace.

"...Thank you, Ma-kun."

"Uh, sure. Are we done yet?"

"Yes. I'm okay now. Mommy's on board."

She let go of him, and her smile was back to normal—filled with love.

"What matters most is how you feel, Ma-kun. That's all Mommy cares about. I will miss...a lot of things. But Mommy wants to be there for you and give you a push into the future. Nobody loves you more than me."

"Okay. Good. Just...promise me one thing. Dad may have started this, but it was my decision. So...don't take it out on him."

"Don't worry about that. I won't. I'll scold him a little later for taking you to that cabaret, but that's all. Hee-hee."

"Y-yeah...you can go right ahead on that one. And Mom..."

"Yes?"

"Thanks for understanding. I'm...really glad you do."

He got on his knees in the water and did a proper thank-you bow. "Oh my! So formal!" Mamako rubbed his head, which felt good.

His wish had been granted. His party was in sync. They knew what they had to do.

So Masato raised his head and turned to face his friends.

"All right, everyone—!"

"Tomorrow's the big fight with the Demon Lord! Let's make it a good one! Woo!"

""""Woo!""""

"Right to the bitter end, huh, Mom?! *I'm* the one fighting! You stay on support!"

Mamako would always be a scene-stealer.

"Okay, all this chatter means we've been in here a long time," said Wise.

"Urgh...my head's spinning..." Porta groaned.

"We're not much better," said Medhi. "It's time we got out of this bath."

"Masato, we're getting out first. You know what to do, right?"

"Sure. Count to two thousand."

The girls got up and left. He watched four backsides sashay away before settling back in the water to count...

"......Hmm?"

Something felt off.

He couldn't put his finger on it. He was in the water, but it didn't feel...buoyant. The problem wasn't him—the water and everything around had gone quiet. No sounds at all. It lasted only for a fraction of a second.

"What was that?"

He had no idea...

Parent and Child Awareness Survey
Adventurer Final Exam Vol. 3

Are you close to your mother?
Very close!

Do you talk with your mother? How often?
We talk a lot!

Has your mother said anything lately that made you happy?
She said I'm more important than anything! That made me so happy!

Has your mother said anything lately that made you unhappy?
She said she had to leave... N-no, never mind! It's for work! She had to go to the real world. I get it!

Do you ever go shopping with your mother?
We don't live together right now, so not often, but once we do, I want to go with her!

Do you help your mother?
Yes! I'll help any way I can!

What does your mother like?
She said she likes me!

What does your mother hate?
Endless meetings!

What are your mother's strong points?
Everything!

What are your mother's weak points?
Nothing!

If you went on an adventure with your mom, would you become closer?
We would!

Answers: Porta

Chapter 4 What's the End of an Adventure Like? ...Thinking About It Put Me to Sleep.

Masato's eyes flew open.

It was far too early. There was only the faintest of lights behind the curtains; the room itself was still dark. But he could feel the impatience stirring within and knew he wouldn't be able to sleep again.

He tried to move, but found warm bodies pinning him down.

Two beds had been pushed together, doubling the size of the sleeping area. Masato was in the center; Porta and Medhi were pressed up against either side of him; Wise was sprawled out over his legs in a legendary display of bad sleep posture. She was rather heavy.

The intent had been a strategy meeting, but sleep had caught up with them, resulting in...this.

I usually wind up in a coffin... I guess this is better, but it still feels like something's missing. Weird.

Doing his best not to wake the girls, he slipped out from under them, looking them over.

Medhi's arms had wrapped around Porta—maybe she was cold. Hug pillow Porta looked rather uncomfortable. Wise was a restless sleeper and did another dramatic roll that nearly drove her off the edge of the bed.

He'd seen them all like this before. That was normal.

But once his battle with Demon Lord Hayato was over, and they'd left the game, he might not see this again.

"...Maybe it'll live on in my memories."

In which case, maybe he should remember them at their best instead. He grinned at the thought, quietly made himself presentable, and left the room.

To face the dawn of his final battle.

*   *   *

The hallway was quiet. There were other guests staying here, but they must've still been asleep.

Keeping his footsteps light, Masato headed toward the smell of miso soup.

"Still all wrong for a fantasy world…" he said with a chuckle as he stepped into the dining room. But he first noticed her in the kitchen.

Mamako—his real mom, who'd tagged along into the game world.

She was humming to herself. What was so fun about making breakfast? As he watched her hustle about, she suddenly turned toward him—son sensor activating.

"Oh, Ma-kun! Good morning."

"Morning, Mom."

"Another early rise? Just a few minutes longer, and I'd have come to wake you!"

"Yeah, I just…woke up. Sorry to let you down."

"Hee-hee-hee. Well, you should be sorry! Mommy's just so mad we couldn't do our little morning routine." Despite her words, she was all smiles. Just like always. "If you want to make up for it, you could give Mommy a smooch on the cheek?"

"In your dreams. Maybe some other day."

"Shame! It'll be a while before breakfast is ready, so you just relax over there."

"Okay, will do."

The menu this morning was rice and miso soup, fried fish, eggs, and pickled veggies. He glanced across the dishes being prepped then took a seat at the table, watching his mother work.

Back to her old self.

Same old Mamako.

He knew he'd be able to watch her cook in their kitchen back home, too. There was nothing special about that. He could see it anytime he wanted.

But he couldn't look away.

"Say, Mom…"

"Yes?"

"Quick question. What was it like when you first tried cooking in-game?"

Mamako didn't turn around, but this little pop quiz made her tilt her head. "I certainly came to appreciate the convenience of modern appliances. Especially rice cookers."

"Ha-ha-ha. Sounds serious."

"It is! I mean, getting rice just right is very tricky!"

"I can imagine. When I start cooking for myself, that'll be the first thing I buy. That and a microwave."

It was an offhanded comment, but Mamako's hands paused on a pickled vegetable, mid-chop. "...Ma-kun, you're going to cook for yourself?"

"Well, yeah, once I live on my own. Whenever that happens."

"How far off do you think that is?"

"I dunno... I mean, first we gotta beat the game and get back to the real world. Then I've gotta focus on school, go to college, find a job...so not for a good long time."

"But you want to? Someday?"

"I'd like to try it out, sure. Kind of a nebulous goal, I guess?"

"Oh..."

Mamako started chopping again. A steady *tap tap tap*. And as she worked, she added, "If you move out on your own, Mommy's going to sneakily follow you."

"That'd defeat the whole purpose."

"Hee-hee-hee. True. It would be the two of us, moving out together!"

"Yeah. Don't make it weird."

"Hee-hee. I'm sorry. Mommy's acting strange today."

She flashed him a happy smile, then focused on her cooking.

And as she did...

...Hngg?

Masato felt something was amiss, just like in the bath last night. It was as if everything around him was sinking—but without sound or shaking. And it felt much more pronounced than the night before.

...Don't tell me...

Once before, when Dark-Mom Deathmother had tried to pry children everywhere away from their parents, the feelings of mothers everywhere had created depressions in the earth and sea all throughout the world.

He worried that Mamako was about to do the same, but...

"La la la...Ma-kuun...is Mommyyyy's...favorite son! Mommy loves Ma-kuuun! La la la! Hee-hee-hee."

The way she was making up a son love song as she cooked sure didn't *seem* depressed. Kinda the opposite. Which was mortifying. He was probably overthinking it.

"C'mon. She's the ultimate mom!"

"Ma-kun? Where'd that come from?"

"Nothing! Never mind."

As they spoke, footsteps came down the hall. "*Yaaawn!*" "Wise, get it together." "Good morning!" The girls were up.

They'd timed it well—breakfast was ready. Mamako proudly showed off the pot of miso soup.

"Everyone's here! Let's eat. The miso soup is extra good this morning!"

The girls all perked up instantly, running over.

Masato rose to his feet, too. "Great! Let's dig in."

He couldn't enjoy these in-game mornings for much longer.

They scarfed down the food, got ready, and left the inn behind.

The roads were still fairly empty.

"Well, Ma-kun? Where do we go?"

"That's...a good question."

Hayato had said he'd be waiting in the "ideal spot," but not given any specifics.

Wise and Medhi were frowning at Masato. Awkward.

"Um...r-right! The item Dad gave me! That oughta lead us there! It better!"

"You are *so* talking out your ass right now."

"It will! Look!"

Masato held up his hand. The Demon Lord's feather appeared.

He thought it would settle on his palm, but a gust of wind caught it and blew it away.

"Huh?"

"Eep!" cried Porta. "It's moving really fast!"

"We'd better run after it, Masato!" said Medhi.

"R-right! Come on!"

The feather was high above the streets of Catharn now, fluttering in the breeze. They ran after it, looking up, full speed ahead.

And as they rounded the corner…

"I'm late! I'm la—augh!"

"Huh? Whoa!"

A girl with a slice of bread in her mouth came rushing from the other side. Impact imminent! "But I'll dodge it in time!" Masato made a deft leap…or tried, but too late—they smacked right into each other.

The girl bounced off him and fell over backward—it was Mone from the Mom Shop.

"Oh, Mone! Man, you scared me."

"Huh? Wh-why do you know my name? Who are you?"

"Who—? Oh, right. Your memories are still sealed…"

"They are? What are you—? Ah! I just remembered!"

"You did? Is this the hand of destiny?!"

"You're the people Ms. Shiraaase brought in a few days ago! Yep, I remember now."

No use. Mone still had no clue who they were. She only knew them as people who'd stopped by the shop once—so she was treating them with professional courtesy.

They'd been so close—this hurt. Masato felt very sad. He wanted only to remind her…but when he looked up, the feather was almost out of sight. They couldn't linger here. Mone would have to wait.

"Sorry to scare you like that, but we're kind of in a hurry! Later!"

"Oh, uh…sure?"

He grabbed her hand and helped her up, then turned and ran away. The girls all gave Mone a sad look and hurried after him.

Nobody they passed had any memories of them. All they got were baffled stares from passersby wondering what all the rush was about.

They'd spent more time in Catharn than anywhere else. There were familiar faces around every corner, far more than in other towns. Usually coming here meant Mamako was instantly mobbed—which was actually rather frustrating.

But today nobody stopped them.

"Ma-kun, before we beat the game, what do you say we take a leisurely world tour?"

"I'm in! Ending it on this note is way too depressing," said Wise.

"There are so many people I want to say good-bye to!" added Porta.

"After the seal on their memories is lifted, we'll have to see everyone again," said Medhi.

"Yeah...good idea."

Masato swore he'd come back...

But for now, they had to chase that feather.

They chased it all the way out of Catharn.

Fearing the Heroic party's levels, the lesser monsters hid in the brushes, coming nowhere near them. Masato wouldn't have minded one last battle to remember them by, but that would have to wait until this was all over.

"Ah, damn it! It's the same color as the clouds! Totally blending in!"

"Porta, your eyes are our only hope," said Medhi. "Make sure you don't lose it."

"Okay! Leave it to—ah! It stopped over the transport point!"

"Great, let's get up there!"

They raced up the stairs to the plateau and the transport circle on it. The feather was hovering in the air above, and the circle on the ground below was pulsing with light—as if in response.

"My Hero senses are telling me...we're about to get transported away!"

"Literally anyone can tell that much."

"Yeah, dumb joke, sorry."

It was final battle time. As the Hero and the party leader, Masato had a duty to make sure everyone was in peak condition.

First, Porta.

"My party's second member, the Traveling Merchant. Porta, you ready?"

"Yes! I have all the items we need! I've got support covered!"

"Cool. Then let's start by using a magic seal cure on Wise; she's probably already affected."

"Got it!"

"I am not!"

Next was Wise.

"Our third addition, the Sage. Wise, you ready?"

"Totally. MP all topped up. My ultimate magic'll blow away any monsters, even your dad."

"Monsters are one thing, but leave my dad to me. Seriously. Are you *sure* your magic isn't sealed? Really? Positive?"

"Why are we so worried about this? I'm fine! My magic isn't—"

"*...Spara la magia per mirare... Tacere.*"

"What the—Medhi! Don't sneak-seal me!"

And then Medhi.

"And our fourth member, the Cleric. Medhi, you ready?"

"Yes. Ready for anything. Leave support and recovery spells to me. Just one thing..."

"Yes?"

"I realize you're doing this in the order we joined the party, but I'm not particularly happy about being called fourth... It's very depressing. *Sigh...* If I'm being put in fourth place, life is not worth living." ... *Rummmble...*

"That's your cue to kick Wise, the impenetrable wall!"

"Ha! Medhi's fourth, and I'm third! That makes me better than—ow!"

Dark power was unleashed upon Wise's shin.

Last but not least was none other than Mamako.

"And my first companion, the Normal Hero's Mother—until she job-changed to Ma-kun's Mommy. Is that right? Well, whatever... Mamako Oosuki!"

"Oh my. It feels so strange to hear you call me by my full name like that!"

"Yeah. Let's fix that: Mom, you ready?"

"Yes, Mommy is completely ready. I'll be cheering you on, Ma-kun. And..."

For a moment, she hesitated.

"...then we'll beat this game and go back to the real world together," she said with her usual smile.

This was how Mamako always was. Nothing to worry about.

Masato nodded and turned toward the transport point. "Let's go."

They were off! The party stepped onto the magic circle and were wreathed in light.

At that exact moment...

In a room not on this earth, filled with consoles—like an air traffic control tower

"Is...this actually possible?"

Demon Lord Hayato and the mothers had gathered and were staring over Dark-Mom Deathmother's shoulder at her screen.

It showed the full map of the game world, with numbers representing the elevation and the sea depths of the terrain. Those numbers were the problem—particularly the latter.

In all oceans, the numbers were regularly diminishing.

"This means...the sea level is sinking, right?" Kazuno asked.

"If that were all, the height of the land would be increasing correspondingly," Medhimama said, shaking her head. "But that isn't budging one bit."

"Then..."

"I can infooorm you the land is sinking at the same speed the ocean is."

Shiraaase was using a personal admin device to collate data.

The game world was composed entirely of data—the land and sea maps were all linked together.

If both were sinking in tandem, then you might assume it was sinking Jenga-like, with one data layer at a time vanishing...

But the more Shiraaase poked at the data, the more puzzled she got. "The total data volume remains unchanged, however. Deathmother, what do you make of this?"

"The sunken sections must be accumulating somewhere. Converted to energy, or aggregated somehow..."

Deathmother tore her eyes off the screen, removed her glasses, and rubbed the bridge of her nose. She laughed softly. "I only know one person who could cause something this absurd... What do you think, Shiraaase?"

"Funny you say that. I was thinking the same thing. This is far beyond the depressions that occurred when other mothers became sad... On the surface, all is well, but the sea and land are sinking, and she's building up reserves of dangerous energy... Your wife is quite a gal."

This last line was definitely a tease.

Hayato managed a brief smile, but it soon faded. "I'd never have stood a chance on my own. Shiraaase, thank you for the timely advice. I was right to ask you all to help. Please, lend me your power. If we don't defeat the ultimate mother's strength, Masato has no future."

That made the four women gulp audibly. After all, they were mothers themselves.

"Shiraaase, wasn't there one more we could call in...?" Hayato asked.

"Don't worry, I've already asked. She wants to adventure with her children awhile longer, so she's still out there—but when the time comes, she'll appear instantly. She can do that."

"Very well. Then we're all ready."

Demon Lord Hayato left the room. The automatic doors slid open, and he advanced down a hall made of sciencey materials to a balcony.

In the blue skies above, he could see the light of a transport spell.

"...There you are, Masato," he said with a grin, ready to face his son.

The blinding light and floating sensation vanished. Masato opened his eyes and beheld the site of their final battle.

"Wow..."

They were in the sky. Everything around them blue. Clouds beneath their feet.

Ahead of them was a city unlike what lay on the ground below. The buildings were futuristic yet weathered—like the ruins of an advanced civilization that had visited this planet in ancient times.

And the entire city was resting on a flying boat. The party had landed on the prow.

Tears gushed from Masato's eyes. "*Gasp!* Dad, you totally get it! Ancient civilizations! Flying ships! Everything I ever wanted!"

"Yeah, yeah, very nice. But, um—*monsters.*"

"Careful!" cried Porta. "There's a lot of them!"

Monsters were already inbound, their ferocious eyes locked on the party, rushing their way.

Flying midsized dragons—a flock of wyverns!

Masato's tears flowed freely.

"Flying enemies! Dragons! Ohhhhhh! My—my whole thing!"

"It doesn't sound like he's going to listen if we tell him to save his power for the duel with his father," said Medhi.

"That's my Ma-kun! Go have fun."

"Oh, you bet I will!"

A kid at their first amusement park would probably be less hyped up. Masato threw himself into the fray, transcending innocence…into imbecility.

But a moment later, he snapped into battle mode.

"Flying enemies are mine! C'moooon!"

Calmly targeting the nearest foe, he swung the Holy Sword Firmamento. It unleashed a shockwave that penetrated the dragon's tough scales and cleaved the beast in two!

The sight of their fallen comrade infuriated the wyverns, and four of them rushed at Masato at once, from all sides.

Masato looked absolutely delighted.

"Don't mess with the Hero of the Heavens!"

He swung his sword horizontally, doing a full 360 spin. The shockwave split, each section forming a hawk that swooped at the incoming wyverns. Sharp talons and beaks tore into their opponents—and the hawks got the wyverns by the throat, hauling them downward and slamming them into the ground. Four foes eliminated as one.

"Hell yeah! Next!"

There were more flying foes coming. Masato readied his next attack, but…

Fearing his strength, the approaching wyverns let out pitiable screeches and fled.

"Huh? Yo, wait! Don't be scared! I mean, I'm flattered, but this also kind of sucks! Come on, fight me!"

His desperate cries proved futile. All the wyverns were soon gone.

"You're kidding, right?! That's it?! Come ooooon! That's not funny! Let me fight some more!"

The wyverns did not return.

But…

"Then I'll take you on."

A figure leapt down from a window in a building ahead. In the blink of an eye, she was right in front of him, a needlelike blade thrust toward him.

Just before it impaled his shoulder, Masato got his own blade up, using the side as a shield.

"Huh? You stopped my attack? Impressive. But I'm not gonna stop to praise you!"

"Wait, you're—!"

The girl in front of him had a tigerlike, ferocious grin.

Amante.

"Oh, Amante! Don't scare me like that."

"Hm? How is it you know my name? All my memories of Masato Oosuki have been sealed away, so I have no idea who you are. Not that I'm going to explain any of that!"

"Mm? Wait."

She'd definitely used his name just now.

Amante took a leap back, rapier pointed at him. "We found this dungeon first! We're gonna enjoy exploring it. I dunno where your little Heroic party came from, but you aren't gonna stop us."

"So you know I'm the Hero… Hey, Amante, are you—?"

"Now scram. Or I'll have to lay down some hurt." She waggled her blade, smiling viciously. And the attack…

Came from his left.

"Yer wide open! Mah!"

"Hey, no fair!"

A tiny kid in a shark hoodie popped out of Masato's blind spot—Fratello.

Her fists, equipped with brass knuckles, were aimed right at Masato's ribs. Caught off guard, his block was too late—!

"I don't think so. *Spara la magia per mirare… Barriera!*"

Medhi's defensive spell activated just in time. A magic wall appeared around Masato, stopping Fratello's blow.

But a third attack was already incoming.

"Here gooooes! …*Spara la magia per mirare… Fusione Nebbiaaaa!*"

"Only one person elongates her words like that!"

He looked up and saw a girl in a skeleton-themed suit riding a giant magic tome. Definitely Sorella.

An ominously colored mist sprang up around him. The moment it touched his hair, the follicles began to melt. "Aiieeee!" At this rate his equipment was going to—!

"Masato, you stay inside the defensive wall! I got this. *Spara la magia per mirare… Forte Vento!* And! *Forte Vento!*"

Wise with the chain casting. A powerful gust of wind blew all the magic mist away.

And the second gust—"Mah?" "Yiiiiikes!"—blew Fratello and Sorella away—"Wai… Gahhh!"—and hit Amante head on.

She'd defeated all three foes.

"Medhi, Wise—thanks. Huge help. Now then…"

"Hee-hee. We clearly need to chat with these ladies."

"Why did you attack us?"

Mamako and Porta joined them, one ready to scold, the other doing big puppy dog eyes.

All three opponents quickly put their hands up in surrender.

"Okay, okay, dumb prank, sorry."

"It was Amaaante's idea! She said we should tease Masato a liiittle."

"This cockamamie scheme was all Sorella. I wanted no part in it, but it was no use. Ya gotta believe me, sonny."

"Yep, I figured as much… Just to be sure, all three of you totally remember us, right?" Masato asked.

Amante puffed up with pride. "Obviously," she said. "Who do you think our mother is?"

"Aha. Hahako undid the seal. That explains it."

Hahako had appointed herself mother to these three—but she was actually a unique being born from the game's main systems. She could rewrite NPC programming with all the ease a regular mother would have rearranging the furniture in her parents' home.

It was a relief to have someone remember them.

These girls had been the party's enemies from the moment each of the trio appeared. They'd caused no end of trouble and fought constantly—so it was ironic that they were the first NPCs to remember the Hero's party.

Masato was smiling despite himself. "Oh... You guys remember us, then! Cool, cool. Ha-ha-ha."

"Yiiiikes. Where did that laugh come from? Soooo creepy."

"...Lost your last marble there, sonny?"

"I'm not creepy! And I've got all my marbles, thanks." He slapped his cheeks, recovering. "So where's Hahako? She's not with you?"

"She's here," said Amante. "She was exploring with us a few minutes ago. But it seems like there's something fishy going on...so she's out handling that."

"Handling what exactly?"

"I dunno." Amante took a quick glance in Mamako's direction and made a face.

The Libere trio got to their feet.

"We'd better go. You guys should head toward Centrale."

"Centrale?"

"Mama Hahako said it's the central building that basically controls everything on the ship... The big one in the middle, easy to find. That's where you'll find your dad, Masato Oosuki. Not that I need to explain that!"

"Thanks for explaining it anyway. But you're not coming?"

"We're the interception squaaaad. So we're on standbyyyy."

"Interception?"

"What could that mean?" Porta asked. "Is there another threat?"

"Y'all are better off not knowing. Just keep yer minds on the throw-down with sonny's old man."

The trio ran off toward the ship's stern. It didn't quite add up, but...

"Come on, Ma-kun! No time to waste. Let's finish this fight and beat the game!"

"Y-yeah, that's the idea…"

Mamako gave him an oddly cheery push, and he started walking.

The monsters they faced were winged insects, birds, dragons—all flying foes.

And flying enemies? "They're miiiiiiine!" "Go for it." Masato was having the time of his life, shockwave after shockwave cutting through the enemies.

As they picked their way through decrepit, crumbling buildings, they saw an extra big one up ahead—like a capless pyramid, or some sort of temple.

Centrale.

"*Hah…hah…* F-finally. Such a struggle to get here…I can barely stand…"

"You're the only one who's tired, Masato," Medhi noted.

"Masato! Have a recovery item! I have water, too!"

"And Mommy's lap pillow is always here for you. Hee-hee."

"I'm gonna pass on that offer, but… Ugh…must fight the urge to nap…"

"Go nap on your mommy's knees…while I get to be the first in!" Wise dashed off, trying to cross the clearing in front of Centrale.

But a dark cloud formed in the skies above, swelling exponentially.

"*Luce della Dannazione!*"

There was a crash of thunder, and a lightning bolt shot toward Wise.

However…

"I saw this coming! …*Spara la magia per mirare… Barriera!* And! *Barriera!*"

Wise's defensive spells activated. Two magic barriers appeared over her head, absorbing the lightning bolt.

She shot a triumphant grin at the Centrale entrance, where the Queen of the Night herself stood—Kazuno.

"Oh? Impressed you noticed."

"This had your stench all over it, Mom. I figured there'd be a trap, and I was right."

"Genya! I do *not* have a stench. Take that back!"

"You reek! You're drowning in cheap perfume! ...So? What do you want?"

"Simple. I'm here to slow you down." Kazuno raised her folding fan and snapped it closed, pointing it at Wise. "Masato's father wants a one-on-one battle with his son. That means you're in the way, Genya. You come play with your mommy."

"Huh. Okay, fine."

Wise returned the gesture, pointing with her magic tome, never once taking her eyes off her mother. "Masato, you go on ahead. I'll handle my mom."

"Wise...you're sure?"

"I got this. We'll just have a little family meeting. Don't you dare lose, Masato."

"I won't. See you later."

No time to nap on Mommy's lap. They left Wise behind, heading inside.

As they passed Kazuno...

"Masato, I know you want to go all out in the battle against your father...but make sure you leave a little energy in reserve. You might need it later."

"Huh...?"

With that cryptic advice from the Queen of the Night, they were inside Centrale.

The party's footsteps faded into the distance.

Wise turned her attention back to Kazuno.

"Well, Mom? Let's get this started. I'm gonna knock you sideways."

"Ooh, how fierce! What's got you so fired up? ...Oh, is this because I was flirting with Masato? Did I make you jealous?"

"Wha—?! Of course not!"

"Don't try and hide it. You've never been this close with any other boys. How cute. You're adorable, Genya! *Snort.*"

Wise lost it completely.

"Okay, shut the hell up right now. Time to get started! ...*Spara la magia per mirare... Tacere!* And! *Tacere!*"

"Ah?!"

Wise's chain casting sealed Kazuno's magic.

Wise's magic was also sealed.

"Wh-what is wrong with you?!" Kazuno shouted. "*My* magic is one thing, but why seal your own?!"

"Simple. With your mom cheats active, I can't beat you in a magic duel. But if I beat you with spells while your magic's sealed, I wouldn't feel like I'd won at all. So..."

"Oh, I get it. You wanna work this out our way, huh? ...Bring it!"

"That's right! Parents and kids need to know when to use body language!"

Kazuno threw her fan. Wise threw her magic tome.

Both lunged at the other, grappling.

"Just so we're clear, me and Masato *aren't* like that! Not in the least!"

Wise with the cobra twist!

"Oh, really? Then I'll just devour him for myself! I mean, his face and figure aren't my style at all, but there's value in youth! He'd make a good appetizer. Oh-ho-ho-ho!"

Kazuno with the backbreaker drop!

"What a load of crap! No way you're that depraved! You're just trying to rile me up, but I'm not falling for it!"

Wise with the figure-four leglock!

"Ah-ha-ha! Too obvious? Just don't let Medhi snatch him from you!"

"I-I...wasn't planning to... Gah?!"

Kazuno with the scorpion death-lock!

Wise's resistance faltered, and Kazuno tightened her hold. "Owwwww!" Wise was in trouble!

But then Kazuno eased off a bit.

"Fine, follow your own heart. It's your life."

"Mom...?"

"Besides, this is hardly the time for personal stuff. Lend me your ear." Kazuno put her arms around Wise's neck from behind—a gentle kind of choke hold. She whispered, "I'm going to teach you the ultimate spell—one of my own creation. Listen and learn."

"Ultimate spell? What for...?"

"You're gonna need some offensive power. The situation is far more dire than you realize. If you want your beloved Masato to have any kind of future, you'll have to fight."

"Beloved, my ass! That's not—!"

"I don't care what it is. You're a girl, yes? Try doing something for a boy for once. I'll make a good woman outta you yet, Genya."

Wise was still struggling, so Kazuno tightened her grip.

"You'll need every last nerve you've got," Kazuno said, her expression grim. "You're up against the very best."

With Wise gone, the party was down to four. They were headed swiftly into Centrale itself.

First, the lobby. It was festooned with monuments to planets and art that had withstood the ravages of time. There was a grand piano along with tea ceremony and ikebana sets—signifiers of high class.

And leaning against the piano was Medhimama—eyes closed, waiting quietly.

Medhi slowed to a standstill. "You three go on ahead."

"You're sure?"

"Yes. Like Ms. Kazuno said, our mothers are here to slow us down. And there's a few things I'd like to speak to my own mother about."

"Got it. We'll go on ahead. Catch up when you can."

Leaving Medhi behind, the party headed farther in.

Silence reigned.

Medhimama's eyes opened, and she smiled. Medhi smiled back.

"...There's something I'd like to say first," Medhimama began.

"What is that, Mother?"

"I was not myself last night. I'm not to blame—the booze was responsible for everything."

"Excuses like that do no one any good." ...Rummmble...

Dark power surged from Medhi's every pore as she raised her staff.

"L-let's just stay calm, shall we?" Medhimama begged. "I *am* calm." Medhi *calmly* raised her staff.

And tapped Medhimama lightly on the chest. Then she came in for a hug.

"I'm kidding," she said. "You're only human, Mother. It's natural you make mistakes sometimes. I don't see anything wrong with that."

"...Thank you. I'm blessed to have such an understanding daughter."

"All I ask in return is that you overlook some of my own blunders."

"Oh? What might those be...?"

"Blunders I may soon make. Relationships are fraught with peril. I'm not exactly scrupulous where Masato and Wise are involved." *Smile*.

"That smile has me worried... How did I raise such a terrifying daughter...?" Medhimama was taken aback, but she then smirked and put her arms around Medhi. "Very well. Do what you think best. But if you make a move..."

"Naturally, I'll win. I won't accept anything less. This is my own decision."

"Precisely what I want to hear. That is who you are."

In each other's arms, mother and daughter smiled.

Then Medhi pulled away, turning her gaze to the educational tools arranged nearby. "So what is the meaning of this, Mother? I've learned all of these before..."

"I prepared them for you. To cultivate your mind and grant unto you a new power."

"A new power...?"

"The power to grant Masato his future. I am not here to stop you, but to teach you what you need... Medhi, listen well."

"Yes, Mother."

"You are prone to unleashing dark, pent-up energy, but I know well that beneath that is a strong, beautiful mind, forged through ceaseless hard work. *That* is the real Medhi. Your true strength. If you can face yourself once more and draw upon that power, you can make it your own."

"My own true strength... Am I even capable of such a thing...?"

"That is up to you. The decision will be yours."

Harsh words, but there was a smile on Medhimama's lips. An

unwavering confidence that her pride and joy—her daughter—could pull this off.

Faced with such faith and adoration, Medhi could say only one thing: "...Mother! I'll do whatever it takes!"

With a look of resolute determination, she took a seat at the piano.

Past the lobby, the three remaining party members reached the base of a broad staircase leading upward. Once again, a mother was waiting for them: Dark-Mom Deathmother. She was on her hands and knees, bowing her head—showing remorse for drunkenly teasing Masato.

But Porta was still hopping mad.

"Mommy!"

"Y-yes?! What is it?!"

"If you don't treat me just like you did Masato, I'll be very mad!"

"Happy to oblige!"

Porta rocketed toward a waiting embrace. Snuggles upon cuddles upon snuggles. Deathmother looked very pleased. Blissful steam was fogging up her glasses.

"Oh, right. I actually have a gift for you as an apology. It didn't turn out very well, but...here."

Dark-Mom Deathmother sheepishly pulled two little sets of doll clothes out of her pocket. Her motherly sewing skills were still a bit rough around the edges, and the threads were loose, but...that was kind of charming, too.

The clothes were just the right size for Piita and Piitamama, the two dolls hanging from Porta's shoulder bag.

"Gosh! They're so cute!"

"These should give both dollies a power-up. What do you say? Do you want to help Mommy put them on?"

"Yes! I'd love to play dolls with you! ...So, um..." Porta turned to Masato and Mamako, looking worried. Naturally, they nodded happily.

"Mom and I'll go on ahead," said Masato. "You have fun here."

"Mommy has to stay with Ma-kun, so don't worry. We'll see you later!"

"Okay!"

Porta plastered herself blissfully against Deathmother. Masato and Mamako took one last look at them and then walked away.

Alone together, they walked side by side up the stairs. Matching pace. For a while, neither spoke.

Eventually, Mamako broke the silence. "Ma-kun..."

"Mm? What?"

"Why don't you ever snuggle up against me like Porta does?"

"Uhhh...real talk, I'm just too old for that now. You gotta cut me some slack there."

He leaned closer, and his arm bumped her shoulder. Like iron to a magnet, Mamako pressed her shoulder into him.

"I suppose this much is normal, right...?"

"Nah, definitely crossing the line. Too much. Pull back!"

"Hee-hee-hee. Sorry. Then how about this?" She put his arm in hers.

"Why?"

"Why not?"

"Please."

"Hee-hee. Shame. But...can we? Just for a minute? I don't know how much longer I'll be allowed to walk arm-in-arm with you."

"It'll happen, I'm sure. Even back in the real world—"

"So you'll go shopping arm-in-arm with me?"

"Erk... W-well...uh..."

Honestly, there were things he could manage *because* this was a game, something separate from real life.

Seeing him wrestle with the thought, Mamako giggled. "I'm really glad we came to this game together and could have all these adventures. Every day was like a dream. Mommy was so happy here."

"Yeah? Well, that's good. It's been wild, but I enjoyed it all, too."

"So..." Mamako stopped, about to say something. But instead, she shifted gears: "So let's treasure these memories. Let's never forget any of them."

They reached the top of the stairs and found themselves in a different kind of lobby. There were elevators at the back, and tables and chairs at the front.

Sitting at one of these was Shiraaase—and Mamako's doppelgänger, Hahako.

"Welcome to Café Shiraaase. I can infooorm you that this café is exclusively for mothers."

"It's been far too long, Mamako. You are a better mother than any of us, so I'm sure you know without me saying it."

Both women looked at Mamako, who let go of Masato's arm.

"Mommy's instincts say Daddy is up ahead. Go on, Ma-kun."

"That's a shock. I figured you'd want to come with me."

"I do! But I can't. This is your fight, Ma-kun. My beloved son is trying to accomplish something on his own. Mommy can't butt in."

"You say that, but you always do that sort of thing. Are you *sure* you're not gonna swoop in at the last second and beat him for me?"

"I won't. You'd be so mad at me! So I swear I'll stay out of it."

"Okay. I'll trust you on that."

He glanced at Shiraaase and Hahako. They nodded—as if to say they'd take care of Mamako for him.

One of them had been helping them out since the game began. The other was a mother as powerful as Mamako herself. He was sure they could handle things.

A few steps farther, and he'd be fighting his father. He took a deep breath.

"I'm ready."

"Good luck!"

Mamako gave Masato a pat on the back, and he stepped onto the transport circle.

At the top of the elevator ride was a garden that stretched out behind Centrale. There were no traces of any remaining vegetation, just the blue sky in all directions—a rooftop garden.

And in the center of it stood Masato's father, a huge cursed sword on his back.

Masato stepped closer, stopping at the tip of the blade's reach.

"'Sup. Your cute kid is here to kick your ass."

"Sheesh, that greeting couldn't be further from 'cute.'" His father—Hayato, the Demon Lord—chuckled. "Let's begin with a question. My beloved son—have you grasped the meaning of the Demon Lord's quest?"

"Yeah, thanks to you. I fell right into your scheme, and that forced me to think about my future. I've made up my mind to beat this game and start the next phase of my life."

"Glad to hear it. But do you have the strength to follow through? I am your final trial, an obstacle you must overcome."

Hayato turned and grabbed Universo—the cursed sword harboring the blackness of outer space.

Masato drew Firmamento—the Holy Sword of the Heavens.

Their smiles faded.

"What future are you dreaming of, Masato?"

"In a word—the best life ever."

"Aha. But I'm afraid that dream must end here."

Hayato's voice took on a nasty edge.

And like it was effortless, he swung his greatsword at his son.

Masato quickly held out his left hand, deploying his shield wall, try-ing to block—but the blow hit hard. He couldn't stand up to it; he was forced backward.

The Demon Lord strode forward, as if he were out for a stroll. Even with both legs firmly planted, Masato's feet slid steadily away.

"Yo, how are you so strong?!"

"This is the power of the Daddy Demon Lord—the result of turning economic might into strength. Power far beyond the Hero Son's!"

"Gah, I ain't that easy! If I put my mind to it...!"

Masato took a big leap back and raised his sword. Focusing his mind, he prepared a mighty swing—unleashing his most powerful shockwave.

The massive shockwave hurtled toward the Demon Lord!

"Oh, crap! Did I overdo it?!" Masato was genuinely concerned.

But Hayato didn't even try to block. The shockwave hit him—and shattered like thin ice. Zero damage.

As Masato gaped, Hayato grinned. "This, too, is the power of the

Daddy Demon Lord. Endurance gained through practical experience, the constant payments of taxes and insurance premiums—all converted to defense! Comprehensive stability guaranteed by good credit."

"What the hell? Who decided that?!"

"You don't get it? Fair enough. This sort of thing is way over your head."

"Gah, now you're just openly mocking me! Look, I get the gist, okay?! ...And my stamina's no joke, either! I've put up with Mom's cosplaying and...and way worse!"

"Oh? Then let's test that."

Hayato raised his blade high. Pitch-black power gathered at the tip, forming a massive magic circle in the sky.

"You've gotta be kidding—you know magic?!"

"This is Daddy Demon Lord's attack—from higher than the Heavens themselves! Can the Heroic Son withstand it? ...*Spara la magia per mirare...*"

A dedicated Dad Spell.

"Punizione del Padre."

Part of the sky gave way to the light of the universe. Countless meteors descended from above, clashing into each other, merging into a giant fist that fell right toward Masato.

No way he could block a meteor. Some things were just impossible. But...

"I'm not gonna lose! I can't afford to!"

Sons had to be stubborn.

Masato steeled his quivering legs, forcing himself to stay put. He readied his defenses.

"I'm gonna overcome this trial, and head toward my future...!"

The meteoric fist slammed home. He tried to withstand it but was easily crushed. What happened next was lost to him.

The sound of the impact, the explosions, everything within the attack's radius was blown away—and he could sense none of it.

However...

Ah, crap... That hurts...

He was still conscious. He could tell he was lying facedown.

Masato had *not* died. It was hard to call his defense successful—but he *had* endured it.

The next thing he knew, he was stuck in the shattered earth at the base of a massive crater.

That was when he heard voices:

"...*Masato!*"

"...*Masato!*"

"...*Masato!*"

Several of them. Wise, Medhi, Porta—and their moms. Even Shiraaase was calling out to him...

"Ma-kun!"

The loudest voice, the one he'd heard more than anyone else's—Mamako.

...How long is she gonna call me that? Even when I'm all grown up?

He winced and turned toward the voice. Mamako looked really worried. She clearly wanted to run to his side but was standing her ground. This was a fight between father and son. She'd promised not to interfere and was keeping her word.

His friends, the mothers, and his father—all staring at Masato.

...I'll look like a chump if I keep lying here.

He moved his arms, and pain shot through him. But he pushed through it, using his sword to pull himself upright. Proving he would not let his opponent keep him down.

Demon Lord Hayato gave him a satisfied nod and aimed the tip of his cursed blade at Masato.

"You did well enduring that attack. However..."

"I know. A single blow left me black and blue. Big talk isn't gonna cover that. Compared to you, I've still got a lot to learn—and I've gotta own that fact."

"A laudable position."

"And I was thinking—where I'm headed, there's gonna be lots of people like you."

"Indeed. I'm but one in a hundred—a thousand...perhaps even

more. Countless people out there I'd never stand a chance against. Do you think you could survive in that environment? Do you think you're capable of reaching out and taking what you want?"

"Honestly, no. But that won't stop me."

Masato raised his Holy Sword and attacked the Demon Lord. The holy and cursed blades clashed—as did the father and son's glares.

"I've made up my mind to head toward my future! And I won't stop now!"

"Easier said than done."

Hayato effortlessly pushed Masato back and took a vicious swipe with his greatsword. Masato got his left hand up in time, and his shield wall deployed—but it couldn't absorb the momentum. He was knocked back but quickly leapt again into the fray.

"Do you have the strength to keep moving forward?"

"I do! These feelings, right here!"

He poured those emotions into the Holy Sword, taking a vicious swipe of his own. The greatsword easily blocked the blow, but Masato kept the pressure on. It got him nowhere, but he kept pushing.

"Just feelings, hm?"

"That's all I've got right now! And I have no choice but to fight with what I've got!"

"Well said. In that case…you'll have to prove how strong those feelings are."

"I will! Beating you is the first step to my future, Dad!"

Both men leapt back, raising their swords to the Heavens. This next blow would decide the outcome. For a moment, all was silent.

And with a roar, both leapt forward, swinging their blades as one. Holy and cursed swords clashed like thunder…!

And snapped in two. Both of them.

"Huh?"

"Oh?"

The broken blades went flying off to who knows where. Masato stood there stunned, and Hayato started laughing.

"Look at that! My stats are far higher, but I see our swords' durability was evenly matched. With no weapons, neither of us can fight on. Which means…"

"Our battle…"

"…is a tie."

"Again…?! Feels cheap, but…not much we can do…"

Masato's last reserves of strength were gone, and he slumped to the ground.

"If you insist on settling things, we can do that back in the real world."

"Yeah…let's do that. But how?"

"By living our lives! What do you say?"

"I dunno how we'd ever pick a winner."

"If you feel like a winner, you've won. Same goes for losing. That's all it takes. What matters is that father and son compete with one another as all men should. That's what I ask of you. It's how things ought to be between us."

"That's the kind of bond you want to have?"

"Exactly. Now, son—you've been largely beaten down by the economic and societal might of your powerful father. Do you still have the courage to wage a battle you have little chance of winning?"

"Puh-leez."

Masato batted aside his father's offered hand and stood up. Now face-to-face, he held out his own hand.

"I'm gonna make you concede defeat one day. Just you wait."

"Looking forward to it. Let's make it a fair fight, son."

"Absolutely, Dad."

Their handshake was quickly becoming a contest of grip strength, but for now—their battle was done. Mamako and the others had been watching breathlessly; they looked very relieved.

And so…

"Well, Masato—it's time for the final battle."

"The heck? Have you lost your mind?"

"Is that any way to talk to your father?"

"Sorry. But didn't we just *have* the final battle? All I gotta do now is beat the game…"

"Therein lies the problem. Before you can do that, you've got to handle the toughest foe of all. Look there."

Demon Lord Hayato pointed upward with both hands.

Masato looked above him…

"…Huh?"

…and saw a pair of very feminine hands.

One made of earth and stone, the other of churning ocean water. These hands covered the sky itself, reaching out to grab the flying ship.

Parent and Child Awareness Survey

Adventurer Final Exam Vol. 4

Are you close to your mother?
Of course we're close, but I don't have to explain that.

Do you talk with your mother? How often?
We're talking before I even realiiize.

Has your mother said anything lately that made you happy?
She said, "Fratello's the manliest of men!"
(No she didn't.) (Absolutely noot.)

Has your mother said anything lately that made you unhappy?
Some hinky crap about me being "cute."
(Yep, she did say that.) (Totallyyyy.)

Do you ever go shopping with your mother?
We go everywhere together, obviously. Including shopping.

Do you help your mother?
I help eat the food she coooks, and I help wear the clothes she waaashes. I do all sooorts of things for her.

What does your mother like?
Spendin' time with her kids.

What does your mother hate?
I guess...being away from us?

What are your mother's strong points?
Being a mom... That's pretty great, if you ask meee.
I totally naaailed this question!

What are your mother's weak points?
She's a bit of a fussbudget. Could stand to cut us folks some slack.

If you went on an adventure with your mom, would you become closer?
I don't need to write this down. Can't you figure that out just by looking at us?

Answers: Amante, Sorella, Fratello

The flying ship fled higher, but the earthen and oceanic hands kept on reaching for it.

"How far are they gonna chase us? Give it up already!" Amante howled, stabbing the tip of an earthen finger as it drew near the stern. The hand was too massive to feel the blow—it didn't even flinch. It just grabbed for the ship like nothing had happened.

"My rapier is all wrong for this... Fratello! Sorella!"

"Mm. On it."

"The interception squad won't be bested that easilyyyy! Fratello cannon, goooo!"

A magic gust of wind fired Fratello at the hand, and she hit it with her ultimate punch. "Mah!" A lucky crit! The explosive impact knocked the fingertip back.

It sent Fratello flying, too.

"Ahhhhhh! She's falling off the shiiip! Lemme go catch herrrr!"

"All yours! ...Argh, the next one's incoming!"

This was the oceanic hand. A torrent of salt water fell from the palm as it loomed above, grabbing for the deck.

Piercing attacks were *clearly* the wrong way to go. "I'm the last person who should be here!" Amante was helpless to fight; all she could do was assume defensive maneuvers.

But then the oceanic hand stopped.

"Huh......?"

"Sorry I'm late. I have forcefully relinked my motherly powers, stopping the attack for now. It will not last long, I'm afraid."

"Mama Hahako! You're here?"

The ground next to Amante warped, and Hahako rose up from it.

She had synched the oceanic hand to her own, holding it in place—but it was clear she couldn't stave it off much longer. It was already moving again—and the earthen hand joined it.

"Argh, what's with these things? If even our mom can't control them..."

"She is completely out of control," said Hahako. "She will not accept emotional input from any other mother. The reserve of energy she had been secretly accumulating has overflowed. We're lucky it did not directly damage this world—but that danger may yet await us."

"Ugh. What a pain!"

"She is the strongest of us. Her power is greater than anyone's, and none of us stand a chance against her. Only the cause can solve this... and that may be wishful thinking."

Hahako glanced back at Centrale with a worried frown.

The top of Centrale was a bridge that doubled as an observation deck, commanding a full view of the surrounding environs. Everyone not on the interception squad was gathered here—and Hayato was at the ship's wheel.

"This is as high as we can get, I'm afraid. From here on out, we just have to maintain top speed and hope. I've got to focus on steering, so if someone else can relay the hands' movements to me..."

"Eep! They're coming after us really fast!"

"Ah, the earth hand's coming in on starboard! Masato's dad, evasive maneuvers!"

"The water hand's closing in on port! You must avoid it!"

"Both sides, huh? Then our only path is down!"

The girls were helping, albeit somewhat chaotically. Hayato sent the ship into a dive. They plunged through the clouds, then swooped low across the ocean's surface.

"Well? Did the cloud cover make them lose track of—?"

"Nope, not for a second! Masato's dad, turn starboard!"

"Wait, Hayato! Don't listen to Kazuno. Port! Hard to port!"

"Hey, Memama! Port's wrong! We gotta go starboard!"

"Calm down, both of you! They're coming from both sides! I'm taking over!" said Deathmother. "I'll access the systems and calculate the best answer— Aaaggghhh?! My tablet battery's dead! Shiraaase, hand me your PDA!"

"I can infooorm you I forgot it somewhere."

"At a time like this?!"

"I can also infooorm you I was kidding and it's right here. Heh-heh-heh."

"Does this look like a good time to be joking?! You're the worst!"

"A-at any rate, they're coming from both sides, so up we go!" said Hayato.

The mothers were helping, although no less chaotically than their daughters. This time the ship swooped upward, back through the clouds. Higher and higher!

But still the hands came after them! They dove and rose and twisted and turned. The flying ship was rocketing around like a roller coaster, veering wildly through the sky—and wreaking havoc on the bridge.

Only two people remained calm.

"You okay, Mom?"

"Yes, Ma-kun. I'm holding on to you! Hee-hee-hee."

"I think this railing would be steadier, but fine."

Mamako was all smiles, snuggling up against Masato, who was vacantly watching the massive hands attack.

"Masato! Why are you being so chill?! And you too, Mamako!" Wise shouted.

"I mean, those hands just…don't feel threatening, y'know? They're actually kinda…gentle, and warm… Mom, you agree, right?"

"I agree with Ma-kun. I don't see a problem if they catch us."

"R-really?" said Medhi. "Well, if Mamako says so…"

"Maybe we don't have to run!" said Porta.

"No…we must. If we're caught, it's all over," Demon Lord Hayato insisted. He glanced at Masato and Mamako and made up his mind. "Masato, listen up. Those two hands are Mother Earth and Mother Ocean—the manifestation of matriarchal power. In other words… Mamako's power."

"Mom's… Oh, I get it. Now that you mention it—I dunno how to put this, but it *feels* just like her."

"And the feelings driving them are Mamako's. Those hands are trying to catch you, Masato—and keep you trapped in this world. They're trying to stop you from beating the game."

"Huh?" Masato gaped at Mamako. She looked baffled. "Trying to stop me...? Mom, you know better. You agreed it was time we finished. You said so!"

"Y-yes, I did. Mommy would never lie to you, Ma-kun. I'm on board with your decision. What matters most is how you feel. So..."

"So you overrode your own emotions?" Hayato asked. "You completely erased any desire you might have to keep playing the game with Masato?"

"W-well..."

Mamako got very quiet. She shot Masato a sheepish look; that made the answer clear.

"Mamako, be honest," said Hayato. "There's a part of you that really wants to catch Masato and keep him here in the game world—isn't there?"

"...Yes. There is."

"Can you control it?"

"I'm sorry—I don't think I can. When you and Ma-kun finished your little fight, I thought, 'Oh, we just have to beat the game now!' and these feelings just came bursting up inside me... Overflowing..."

"Gah?! Now more hands are spawning!" Masato yelped.

"Masato's dad! We've gotta hurry!"

"They're getting stronger! We know what that means!"

Wise and Kazuno had yelled at once, and when everyone looked back—there were now twice as many hands.

Dark-Mom Deathmother was peering at Shriaaase's PDA, gulping audibly. "This is so bad. So much land and sea getting converted to energy and funneled into those hands. Soon the world won't have any land or sea left!"

"It'll be the end of this world. Hahako has informed us that they're not accepting interference from other mothers—unless Mamako herself can get her emotions under control, there's no stopping things. I wish I could infooorm you otherwise."

"It's all my fault… I'm so, so sorry… Really, I am."

A tear rolled down Mamako's cheek, and she buried her face in her hands.

This was all caused by the greatest mother's unbridled love for her son. No one could blame Mamako for it. But neither could they offer words of consolation. Silence settled over the bridge.

But as Masato worked out what was going on…

"*Snort*… Ah-ha-ha-ha!"

…he burst out laughing.

"Ma-kun?"

"It's just…this is the most Mom thing ever."

"Is it?"

"Mom, you've always been *so* selfish. I ask you not to stand so close, you do it anyway. I tell you not to hug me, you hug me harder… You're way more chained to your mom instincts than you think you are. And it's because you're so true to that side of you that your mom powers are this strong, and you can pull off all this crazy stuff and always get your way. That's who you are!"

"I-I don't think—"

"Trust me. That's how we got here! Right?"

"Well…I suppose…" Mamako started hanging her head again.

"Wait, wait. Don't get me wrong. I'm not blaming you here. Okay?"

Masato cupped her cheeks with both hands and then squeezed, giving her a silly face. He lifted her head back up.

Then he looked silly-faced Mamako right in the eye.

"Mom, that's exactly how I want you to be. That's just who you are, as my mom. I hate to say it…but ultimately, this is all because you love your son *so damn much*."

Deeply mortified though he was, his brain about to fizzle out, Masato still hung in there.

Silly-faced Mamako gave him her brightest smile, nodding. Love is selfish.

"Mommy loves you, Ma-kun. I love you so, so much!"

"Okay, thanks. So we know you're gonna be selfish like that… But that works out just fine for me."

"It does?"

"If you're selfish all the time, that means I get to be just as selfish. It goes both ways, right? It's time we had a selfishness duel."

"A duel? Ma-kun and Mommy?"

Masato nodded and let go of her cheeks. He faced her down.

"Mom. I'm gonna beat this game and head toward my future." A stern declaration.

Mamako stared back, just as serious. "Mommy would love to support you in that…but adventuring with you has just been far too wonderful. This game has brought me such joy that I don't want to stop. I don't want to let you beat it. That's how Mommy really feels."

"And thus, the world's in crisis. I've gotta clear the game as soon as possible and force my way out from under your smothering love. That's *why* I need to beat this game."

"I really *am* sorry for all the trouble I'm causing… Oh, I know! If you promise not to beat the game, I'm sure I'll be able to control my feelings again. Then we can have a nice long think about the future together—over the next decade or two, here in the game."

"We're getting nowhere with this… You've left me with no choice!"

"Which of us is more selfish, then? Ma-kun or Mommy? Now that's a real duel."

Who would win? The child who wanted to stretch his wings and fly toward the future? Or the mother who wished to cling to the joy she had here in this game?

Masato vs Mamako. The honest-to-goodness final battle.

The strongest mother against her own son. Everyone watched anxiously…

"First, Mom, I need a favor."

"Oh? What is it?"

"I need you to agree to some handicaps."

"Wha—Masato, you're cheating already?!"

"Can it, Wise. I'm not cheating! I'm making a smart decision based on analysis of combat ability." He put her in a headlock to shut her up. "Sorry, Mom. But if I wanna win, I gotta play smart. First, the red girl, Medhi, and Porta—all three of them are on my team. You girls on board with that?"

"Okay, okay. No way you'd win on your own, so I'll lend a hand."

"I'll help, too. Masato doesn't have a chance in a million of winning otherwise."

"You don't *both* need to make that point."

"I really get how Mama feels! But I promised I'd help Masato! So I'm on Team Masato!"

"Glad to have you. Also, Dad, can I count you in, too?"

"That was always the plan. And because I knew this might happen, I called in powerful allies." Demon Lord Hayato gave the signal...

And Kazuno, Medhimama, and Dark-Mom Deathmother all surrounded Mamako, smiling.

"Oh my! All three of you are mothers, so does that mean you're on my side?"

"We're moms, sure...but we're here to keep you in check," said Kazuno. "When it came time to let your son free, I figured you wouldn't take it well."

"We're the only people who can take you on," said Medhimama. "Nobody but us can do it. Nobody."

"The plan is to have a lot of fun, just us mom friends, and help distract you from Masato! ...And while we're at it, what say we form an idol group with all four of us?"

"Saorideath! If you say another word, I'll end you!" *Grrr!*

"What's done is done! Those memories stay sealed!" *Hiss!*

"S-s-s-sorry!!"

Dark-Mom Deathmother suddenly found herself cowering before two ferocious beasts...but at any rate, all three moms were on Masato's team.

Outside, Hahako and her daughters were intercepting like mad. Masato figured that meant they were on his side, too.

So this was actually Mamako vs everyone else.

"Okay, I'd say that's balanced enough."

"Goodness, Ma-kun! You're so ruthless!"

"I'm up against *you*, Mom. Gimme this one at least. So! The sides are set, but…we still haven't figured out the most important thing!"

"That's right. How do you go about beating the game, Ma-kun? If we don't figure that out…well, I'd be totally fine with it. Hee-hee-hee."

"I wouldn't! Which means…infooorm away, Shiraaase!"

At his call…

The mysterious nun stopped twiddling her thumbs at the edge of the deck and stood up.

"Heh…and here I thought you'd forgotten about me. Now it's my chance to shine! Without Shiraaase's infooormation, you are certainly one helpless Hero. Very well. I shall offer my guidance."

"Please do. How do we beat the game?"

"Masato, the Hero chosen by the Heavens, can only return to the real world through the transport point located in Heaven's Ruins."

"Heaven's Ruins… The place with the doors that wouldn't open because my job had bugged out?"

"Shall we head straight there?"

"No time to waste! Make it happen."

"That will lead directly to beating the game. Are you sure?"

"Yep. That's the goal."

"Understood. Then I have one last piece of infooormation for you—and everyone else. Listen closely."

Shiraaase looked extremely serious all of a sudden. Everyone held their breath. She gazed at each face in turn then closed her eyes.

"The game known as *MMMMMORPG* (working title) is currently a beta build—the final testing phase. The results of this final test will lead directly to the start of the official launch. And that final test—is drawing to a close."

"What did that final test involve?"

"It began with the introduction of the Demon Lord, Hayato. Everything since had been part of the test. A child who has deepened their family bonds by playing this game—in this case, Masato—must desire a future beyond the end of the game itself. Our goal was to see if he could actually take the steps necessary to beat the game. After all, the government can hardly agree to something that would contribute to childhood video game addiction."

"So if I win this Oosuki family duel and beat the game—your test is a success."

"Indeed. The game will proceed toward the official launch—and corresponding to that will be the end of the beta test."

The end.

Everyone gulped.

"This version of the game world will be carried over into the final release," Shiraaase continued. "However, do not assume that any of you will be allowed to adventure here again."

"Wh-what does that mean?" Porta asked.

"The reason is simple. This game is designed for mothers and their children to enjoy together—with the goal of solving any problems they're experiencing. None of you have any significant frictions with your parents anymore—so you no longer qualify to participate."

This left everyone speechless. The moment Masato beat the game—it was over for all of them. He had to think about that one.

"Masato," Shiraaase said, "beating this game is the end of your adventure. You can never come back to this world. Will you still head to Heaven's Ruins?"

Those eyes of hers never wavered—least of all now. He could feel his friends staring at his back.

And so…

"I will," he said. "I've made my choice. It's time for me to move on."

Masato was past hesitating. He turned around, and his friends nodded. They agreed with him.

Mamako looked rather disappointed, but…she soon smiled. "I appreciate your feelings, Ma-kun. Now then…"

She drew both her swords. In her right hand, the Holy Sword of Mother Earth—Terra di Madre. In her left hand, the Holy Sword of Mother Ocean—Altura.

"Uh, M-Mom? Why are you…?"

"Hee-hee. Mommy means business. Ma-kun—let's fight!"

Terra di Madre emitted a crimson glow, and Altura a deep blue one. Each light grew so bright, Mamako herself vanished from view…

And when the two lights faded, there was no sign of her.

"…Huh?"

Mamako had disappeared.

Leaving the Demon Lord Hayato on the bridge to steer the ship, everyone else moved to the prow. The plan was to disembark as soon as they reached their destination.

The ship was headed toward Heaven's Ruins, flying steady and low. The two giant hands were no longer in pursuit.

"...The calm before the storm, huh?" Masato said.

Everyone nodded, looking tense. It was very quiet. The sky was blue. The breeze felt good.

"Oh! Hahako and her children are here!" Porta said. She'd been on lookout and had spotted them rushing up from the stern.

When they arrived, they appeared uninjured but exhausted. All of them were panting as they sat down heavily.

"Rest up. How'd it go?" Masato asked.

"It didn't go," Amante replied. "None of our attacks did squat. Impacts managed to knock 'em backward, but that's it—and they never actually tried to hurt us. It was like they were toying with us."

"I'd say we were dancing on the palm of her haaaand...but we never engaged with anything but the fingertiiiips."

"Total lovey-dovey stuff. When I fell off the ship, she even scooped me up!"

"Yeah, that's mom power for ya. Makes sense those hands would be that doting," said Masato. "Hahako, what's the situation now?"

"Both hands have vanished and show no signs of returning. I'll take a look and see if I can learn anything else—one moment."

Hahako held a palm toward the distant land, concentrating. Then she frowned.

"That's odd. I have duped admin privileges and should have full access, but I can't seem to connect... Perhaps control has been wrested away at a higher tier? ...Deathmother, do you have any ideas?"

"We never implemented access privileges above the admin level. But I'm also locked out. This is so nuts, you have to laugh." Dark-Mom Deathmother gave up poking at her tablet and threw up her hands. Everyone knew who was behind this.

So they all turned to look at Masato. They had one silent question: *What the heck is your mom up to?*

That's what *he* wanted to know. Best to ignore them.

"Yo, Dad! How's the flight going?" he yelled, turning toward Centrale.

"Just dandy! We should reach our destination shortly. If nothing untoward happens." The answer came over the ship's speakers.

Almost there—*unless.*

"...Something's *definitely* about to go down, then."

And no sooner had the words left his lips...

"Maaaaa-kuuuuuun..."

There came a sweet-sounding voice, like she was talking to a baby. Mamako's voice was echoing across the ship's deck.

Everyone braced themselves, looking around—but there was no sign of her.

"Did I keep you waiting? I'm sorry. It took me ages to get ready."

"Nah, you're good. So? Where are you?"

"Hee-hee-hee. Good question. Can you find me, Ma-kun? Mommy's playing peek-a-boo!"

"What am I, a baby?"

"Don't you remember, Ma-kun? This was how Mommy always made you laugh back when you were a baby. No matter how hard you were crying! ...Peek-a..."

A pause. Then...

"...boo!"

Mamako's hands left her face, revealing her smile.

That face was in the sky above the ship—the entire sky.

"..............Hah?"

Mamako's face, so big she could easily swallow a flying ship with an entire city on top. She looked just like she always did, but far beyond giant—more like the myth about the Titan who carried the sky on his back.

"What do you think? Mommy fused with Mother Ocean and Mother Earth and got *thiiiis* big. Now I'm MegaMommy! Hee-hee-hee."

"Aughhhhhhhhhhhhhhhhhhhhhhhhhhhhhhhhhhhhhhhhhhhhhhh-hhhhhhhhhhhhhhh!"

This was the ultimate mom skill, activated when a mother's instincts perfectly melded with those of the earth and ocean—A Motherly Trinity.

MegaMamako appeared!

Masato was still screaming. Even Hahako and Shiraaase's jaws had dropped so hard they almost dislocated. Actually, the shock knocked Shiraaase over—she hit her head, died, and was replaced by a coffin.

No matter how many times he blinked, MegaMamako was still there.

"Well, Ma-kun, let's find out what happens first! Will you beat the game...or will Mommy catch you?"

"Uh, no, waaaaait!"

"Let's go! When you were little, we always used to chase each other around! And Mommy never lost, not even once! I'm gonna get youuu!"

MegaMamako reached out her incredibly huge hands, trying to scoop up the flying ship!

"D-Dad! Daaaad! Full speed ahead! Noowwwwww!"

"Aye-aye!"

The fateful battle began.

The flying ship shot forward at speeds so great, the hull creaked. MegaMamako smiled, easily keeping up. She reached out her arms to catch the ship and Masato on it, to cradle it to her chest.

"Crap, crap, crap! She's gonna catch us! Only one option, then... Kazuno! Medhimama! Deathmother! Please!"

When in doubt, ask a mom.

"What do you want *me* to do? Okay, sure, I said we'd keep in her in check, but not *this*! ...Memama, I bet you can handle it."

"Huh? Kazuno, what's that supposed to mean? You can't just say anything that crosses your mind! We all have our limits, and dealing with a Mamako this big is mine! ...Well, Hotta can handle it, I'm sure. After all, she is Dark-Mom Deathmother."

"That's not a valid reason! Don't rope me into this mess! ...B-but... no matter how big she is, it's still Mamako, so..."

Deathmother spawned the Traveling Merchant's unique equipment—the magic shoulder bag. It opened its monstrous maw, spewing items. Specifically, tea and cookies—big enough for MegaMamako.

"Mamako! Tea's ready! Will you join us?"

"Uh, Hotta? No way that'll work—"

"Oh, how lovely! Don't mind if I do."

"Yikes. She totally bit."

MegaMamako picked up the teacup and a cookie. Both her hands were full! She couldn't catch Masato now.

"Nice, Deathmother! Thanks for that!"

"No matter how big she gets, Mamako is still herself. That's the key to victory! Keep your wits about you. Masato, I'm sure you can handle this."

"Okay! I'll try."

A mom-along adventure had certainly left him with a wealth of mom knowledge. He knew all the things that could distract his mother.

"Yo, Mom! Got a sec?"

"Yes, Ma-kun? What is it?"

"I was just wondering if you'd done any laundry today."

"Laundry? Did I...? Oh dear! That *is* a question... I usually hang it out to dry at the inn—is it still hanging out there? Or did I take it in last night...? Oh my! I just don't remember. Which is it...?"

MegaMamako stopped in her tracks, trying to remember.

Success! The flying ship gained valuable distance.

"Okay, this is working! ...Dad, how much farther?"

"We're close! I can see our destination! Look up ahead!"

When they did, they saw a sheer cliff stretching to the clouds above.

"Still a ways out... Porta, can you see more?"

"Yes! That's the stairs we climbed! I can see the door that wouldn't open!"

"Cool. Then that's Heaven's Ruins, all right. I don't wanna do that climb again; let's hope we can restart from the door. What do you think, Dad?"

"This ship has a hovering function, so we can pull right up alongside."

"Awesome."

The ship gained altitude, emerging through the clouds. Not long after, Masato's eyes could make out the shape of the door. If nothing else happened, then…

But something did.

"Oh, right! I finished the laundry last night. I was all worried about nothing! And I've finished the tea. The cookies were lovely!"

Mamako was back in action. She set the teacup down on a nearby island and was hot on the group's heels once more. It took her only a few steps to catch up.

"How are you so fast?! That's not even fair!"

"Hee-hee. MegaMommy has megalegs! I'm sorry, Ma-kun, but this game of tag is all over. I'm gonna get you!"

"No you're not. I know how to handle you now! …Moms, take it away."

"We've got this. At least, this time anyway. Ready, Memama?"

"I'd rather stay out of it, but very well. I'll work with you this once, Kazuno."

Kazuno struck an aggressive, daring pose, and Medhimama an elegant, confident one.

"Mamako, let's have a nice chat, shall we?"

"Mom talks are a mother's delight. Our one indulgence. I can't imagine you would refuse."

"Oh my! What should I do? I have to catch Ma-kun, but…I *am* curious. I think I can spare a minute… Just one!"

"Certainly. Heh-heh-heh… But mom talks never end. We can keep her here for an hour or two…"

"So? What's this about?" MegaMamako asked.

"It's, um…"

Medhimama looked at Kazuno, who blinked and looked at Medhimama. Medhimama then blinked back at her. Neither of them could think of anything.

"Gosh! Nothing at all? Then I guess we'll have to catch up later."

MegaMamako smiled and looked back at Masato. "The heck?!" Operation: Mom Chat failed! Masato was in trouble…!

"W-wait! Mamako, wait! I have a topic! Don't go yet!"

"Oh, Kazuno? What is it?"

"Um, um…the, uh…the thing! Right!"

Words came tumbling out.

"My dumb daughter said she promised to marry Masato. What are your thoughts on that?"

Of all things.

""Whaaaaaaaaaaaaaaaaaaaaaaaaaaaaaaaaaaaaaaaaaaaaaaaaaaaaaaaaaaaat?!""

Masato and Wise's shrieks were in perfect harmony.

"Yo, Wise, why would you say that?!"

"I didn't! Mom just made that up! …Gawd, Mom! What's *wrong* with you?!"

"Aw, calm down. Look, it proved super effective against Mamako."

"Oh my! Oh my goodness gracious! Oh my heavens! She did? They did? Ma-kun and Wise? Oh my oh my oh my!"

MegaMamako was befuddled! She stopped dead in her tracks.

"Ha-ha! See? That's mom power for you."

"Get off your high horse, Mom! This isn't a joke!"

"Oh, be quiet. We just have to get her in a tizzy about her kid. That's what mom talks are all about! …Memama, you're next."

"Very well. I'm in this to win." Medhimama gave Medhi a quick look.

Medhi smiled and nodded. She was totally on board.

"Mamako, if I might interject? My daughter insists she has a prior claim on Masato's hand."

"Ohhhhh?! Medhi was first?! And then Wise?!"

"Yes. He's two-timing! And that's hardly right. I think this calls for a parent conference!"

"Y-y-yes, indeed it does! We have to talk this out right now!"

MegaMamako was beside herself! Her mind was so preoccupied with marriage, she'd completely forgotten about catching Masato.

This version of Operation: Mom Chat was a success.

"So many problems with this but…at least it looks like we can get there safely," said Masato. Everyone else thought as much, too.

Until…

"Kazuno! Medhimama! I need every last detail! Tell me everything you know!" MegaMamako grabbed the ship with both hands, pulling it to her ear.

They were caught.

"Huh? ...Aughhh!"

"See? Your dumb plan totally backfired!" Wise yelled.

"B-but...we did distract her! We did our job! Right, Memama?"

"Y-yes! This is...exactly what we wanted! We'll keep her busy chatting about this. Hotta, could you get us some tea?"

"I don't know what else I'd do. Masato...good luck."

Kazuno, Medhimama, and Dark-Mom Deathmother ran off toward Mamako...and away from their daughters.

"Good luck? With *what*?! ...Dad? Can we wriggle free?"

"I'm afraid not. I've got it floored, but she's not budging!"

"Crap. We're so close, too!"

Masato could clearly make out Heaven's Ruins, but no amount of long jumping would get him there. They were high in the sky, the ground miles below. Without flight, they'd never get anywhere.

"Mwah-ha-hahhhh! This is the job for meeee!" Sorella hopped on her giant magic tome, floating upward.

"Glad one of us can fly! Thanks, Sorella!"

"Suuuure. Come on! All aboooard!"

"No telling what's up ahead," said Amante. "The interception squad's coming, too!"

"Mm. Ya can't leave me behind, sonny."

"We're coming, too, duh."

"Of course. Till the bitter end."

"Yes! I'm on my way!"

The tome was something like three by six feet, and seven people had just jumped on.

It dropped like a stone.

"Too heavyyy! I can't flyyy!"

"Yeah, I figured," said Masato.

"Masato and I are maaandatory. Maybe two moooore? Who'll it beee? Masato, you chooooose."

"Two more..."

Who would he take to the last dungeon?

There might be monsters in Heaven's Ruins. Combat considered, he should probably take Wise and Medhi. "...Masato..." Porta knew she'd be left behind and looked very sad.

Maybe he should leave his main party and take Amante and Fratello. "Hmmm?" Wise was cracking her knuckles. "You know exactly who to choose, don't you?" Medhi was doing her most terrifying beautiful girl smile. Nope. That option would be fatal.

"Um, gimme a sec. This is super hard! I dunno!" Every option left someone out. Masato was clutching his head.

But...

"Masato, a moment?"

Hahako stepped in—red light on her right hand, blue on her left.

"Hahako, that light..."

"This is a portion of the motherly power fueling Mamako—the opposite of her desire to keep you here. This light is her desire to push you forward."

This was a move designed to give a child courage—the mom skill **A Mother's Push.**

The feelings from their hug had been real. She *did* want to help him, too. These two desires were contradictory, but both a part of Mamako nonetheless.

It was just a question of whether she knew it or not... MegaMamako was still busy chatting with the other moms.

"Sheesh, being a parent is hard, huh?"

"Very. But in her stead, I entrust this to you. Accept it."

Her smiling face just like Mamako's, Hahako put her hands on Masato's back. The light suddenly burst, then scattered and took the shape of a bird's wings.

Masato grew pure white wings.

"I've got wings...?! Holy crap!"

"Time to flee the nest. Go on, Masato."

"Y-yeah... I'll spread my wings...and fly...!"

It wasn't hard. All he had to do was picture it, and the wings on his back began to flap. Masato left the ground.

"Whoa!" Porta shouted. "Masato! You're flying!"

"Hey! How *dare* you be cool!" Wise yelled.

"I'm seeing things," said Medhi. "I must be weary."

"This is real, dammit!"

"Well done. Now then. Wise, Medhi, Porta—these are from your mothers." Hahako summoned new lights, touching each girl's back in turn. All three of them grew wings and floated into the air.

"Wooo! I'm flying! Damn, this is awesome!"

"Masato, your heroines have all become angels. Feel free to lavish praise upon us."

"They really are kinda angelic looking, so…I dunno what to say."

"W-wait! I can't actually fly! Augh!"

Porta's wings were on the small side. Perhaps Dark-Mom Death-mother secretly didn't want her flying the coop just yet. She couldn't flap right—so Wise and Medhi each took a hand. The three of them together could fly just fine.

Now all four of them were soaring free.

Hahako's daughters looked a bit jealous, but they had to settle for riding the giant tome. They deliberately made it fly higher than Masa-to's party so they could look down on them.

"Fine, fine. You sure look like you're having fun, not that I need to point that out to you. Just don't let it go to your heads," said Amante. "Now that we're all flying, we'd better head straight to these ruins."

"Oh, right…," Masato replied. "Okay, Hahako! We're heading out!"

"Understood. I hope you don't mind that I give my final farewell."

"Final…? Oh…"

"Yes. I exist only in this game. Once you beat it, we shall never meet again. So this is our last parting."

With a hint of melancholy, Hahako cast her eyes downward—but then, just like Mamako herself, Hahako beamed, undaunted.

"I am grateful for everything you did for me. There is much I would like to say—but I have no time to say it. Instead, let me promise you this—I won't forget these feelings, or the time we spent together. Even if everyone in this world forgets, I never will. Ever."

"We won't forget you, either. I promise we won't."

"Thank you… Then go on. Take care. And be good to your mothers."

"Yes! We will! Hahako, thank you so much!"

The Hero's party bowed.

And then Masato flew away from the ship. Wise and Medhi pulled Porta after them, the tome riders close behind. They all headed for Heaven's Ruins.

Hahako stood still, watching them go.

The group flew straight to the ruin doors, bypassing the endless staircase, restarting right where they'd gotten stuck before—or at least, that was the plan.

"Sage Wise! Cleric Medhi! What are you doing?" Amante shouted. "You're dropping steadily! Don't you know how to fly?!"

"Oh, shut up! We're flying as hard as we can!" Wise shouted back. "But yeah, we're losing altitude, and I have no clue why!"

"Our wings are fueled by motherly power... Perhaps the farther we get from the source, the weaker they get?" Medhi wondered aloud. "B-but this means..."

"We're going to fall into the ocean!" Porta yelled.

"Nope! Don't worry. You've got the Hero of the Heavens with you!"

With the power the Heavens had bestowed in him, Masato could keep the whole party flying! He drew the Holy Sword, Firmamento...

But it was broken.

"Ohhh, right, it died a noble death in the battle with Dad. Ha-ha!"

"The hell are you laughing for?! We're free-falling here!" Wise hollered. "Augh, that water's coming up faaaast!!"

"What a pickle. Sorella, help 'em out."

"Fiiiine. *Spara la magia per mirare... Forte Ventooooo!*"

"No, not—!"

Just before Masato and his party hit the water, an explosive gust of wind hit them. It caught their outstretched wings, and all four were flung—

—right to the base of the stairs leading up to Heaven's Ruins. "Gah!" Masato hit the ground first.

Then—"Hngg!"—Wise, Medhi, and Porta all landed beautifully on top of him.

Finally—"Hngah?!"—Amante, Sorella, and Fratello all jumped down on top of him, too. Not quite the recovery they'd hoped for, but…at the very least, they were on dry land.

"Eep! Sorry, Masato!"

"It's f-fine… As long as you're safe, Porta…"

"'Kay, Masato, forward march," Wise ordered.

With six girls on his back, Masato crawled up the stairs. "Nope, that's physically impossible." Everyone got off.

He glanced toward the water and saw MegaMamako clutching the flying ship. She had both hands on it, and all her attention was on the chatting moms. Didn't look like she'd seen the rest of them fly away.

"No telling when she'll notice us," said Masato. "Let's get climbing. Full speed to the doors above."

They started moving toward the clouds and the door beyond, running up the stairs.

"Oh! Careful! Monsters incoming!" Porta always spotted them first.

A flock of wyverns was quickly approaching.

Battle time.

"All right! Flying enemies are—"

"Masato? Did you forget again?" Medhi asked.

"Sorry. I'm weaponless." *Slump.*

"Psh. You just stand there and watch, then," Amante scoffed. "We'll take care of them."

"We got this one, sonny."

"Feast your eyes on the three Hahako sisters' teamwoooork."

No sooner had the words left their mouths…

…than Amante broke into a run. So fast, she ran straight up the cliff face into an aerial spin that placed her above the wyverns. "Hmph!" Rapier thrusts like torrential rain pummeled all foes into a downward spiral—

Where Fratello stood waiting. "Mah!" A disarmingly cute battle cry, but her fists sent foe after foe flying.

As for Sorella… "Get theeeem!" She was spawning skeleton armies beneath her tome, and they were swarming any wyvern survivors. Brutal.

The battle was over in a flash.

The wyvern swarm was defeated!

The three Hahako sisters turned toward the Hero's party.

"Sage Wise, Cleric Medhi, Traveling Merchant Porta, and Masato Oosuki. What do you make of our combat performance? Your evaluations, please."

"Why…? Okay, sure," replied Masato. "I mean, I legit thought, 'Damn, they're good.'"

"Are you guys, like, way stronger than before?" Wise asked.

"I thought the same," Medhi added. "Although maybe just mildly stronger. Not very much."

"Arghhh… You can't say anythiiing without being a little snot, Medhi. I guess that's just you being youuuu."

"I thought you were great! Amante, Sorella, Fratello, you're all amazing!"

"Mm. You're a peach, Porta."

"Thanks, everyone. Yes—we're all strong," said Amante. "And we got this strong by fighting you. In other words, this is the strength you gave us. But I'm not gonna admit to that!"

"If we take that further, this is something you'll be leaving behiii-ind. That and us becoming Hahako's daughterrrs. It's all because of youuuu."

"And that'll all stay put. Not just our ol' lady Hahako. We'll remember y'all, too. Ain't no way we could forget."

"So, uh…well, there you have it."

Speech over, the three of them turned and headed up the stairs. Not too fast; one step at time. As if they were savoring their last moments together.

Masato and the girls felt the same way. They followed.

"Hey, Amante…"

"What, Sage Wise?"

"Watch your feet. One false move and you'll go tumbling down. Bruise yourself again."

"I'm afraid the bruise we got when we first met has long since faded." Amante proudly smacked her butt. With a satisfying crack.

"Sorella, your back is wide open. Anyone could land a hit!"

"Mwa-ha-hahhh. You say that, but you don't even want to hit meee. You're a proper lady, Medhiiii. You don't need to force yourself to keep the dark power things going, you knooooow."

"I will if I want to." Medhi tapped her staff on Sorella's back. Sorella wriggled as if that tickled.

"Um, Fratello! Thank you for being so nice when I was one of the Four Heavenly Kings!"

"Mm, I was plumb tickled to get a li'l sister. Was nice bein' a big brother for a spell!"

"Um...but you're a girl, Fratello, so more like a big sister—"

"You fool! I'm a man!"

"Eep! S-sorry."

Fratello straightened her tiny, clearly feminine back, standing bolt upright, and doing her best "manly" walk. But a few steps later, she slowed down.

Fratello had pulled up alongside Masato. She had the shark hoodie pulled low over her eyes, so he couldn't see her face...but could hear her sniffing.

A delicate little fist tapped him in the ribs.

"I'm a man, and men don't waste words. So I'll just say one thing: I'm glad we met."

"Yeah, Fratello. I'm glad we met, too." He reached out and rubbed her head, and got another elbow jab in return.

"One farewell isn't neeearly enough. Let's all make a playyyy." Sorella clung to Masato's other arm, staring up at him with her bewitching, languid eyes. "It's our last chaaaance. Let's have one final rooound."

"Gambling again? Fine! I'm in. What are we betting on?"

"Ummmm...well...hmm. Good questiooon... I had so many ideas, too... Where'd they gooooo...?"

Sorella trailed off into silence. Face buried in her hands, she moved away from Masato...and threw her arms around Wise and Medhi. They patted her trembling back.

Before they knew it, they'd reached the stone doors.

Amante had been in the lead. She stopped, stepping sideways so Masato could pass—but she didn't turn around.

"I hear this door only opens for the Hero. Seems like a fitting end, Masato Oosuki! Prove you're this so-called Hero after all."

"I'd be glad to. I'll show you I'm the best Hero around! At least, the best normal one."

He stepped up to the door. There was a low rumble, and the door swung open. The path had opened for the Hero.

"See, Amante? It *did* open."

"Apparently. So go on! Head in. This is as far as we go. Plus, *she's* catching up."

There was a lot of noise coming from down below.

A mass of earth, and a mass of water, each shaped roughly like human hands. If you squinted, you might think they were modeled after Mamako's—but neither was exactly maintaining form.

"Looks like those are the remnants of Mother Earth and Mother Ocean. Only a matter of time before they relay intel back to Mamako Oosuki. Won't be long before she comes running. You'd better get a move on."

"Okay. Also, Amante…"

"Just—! Go on in!"

She wouldn't even look at him.

Sorella was in tears. Wise and Medhi were crying with her as she pushed them forward. Fratello had tears streaming down her cheeks, and she did the same to Porta (who was also sobbing). The girls were all pushed through the door.

Amante slapped Masato's back, and he, too, was inside.

The door began to close. This was good-bye.

"Amante!" he shouted.

"I said, just *go*!"

Just before it closed, with only a crack left visible—she finally turned around.

"I want to say, 'See you again,' but I can't say that, can I? And I'm *definitely* not about to say 'Good-bye!' I don't even know what else I *can* say! …So just go on in, you dumb Hero!"

She tried to grin but was crying too hard—and then she vanished from sight.

*　　*　　*

Masato stared at the closed door for a long minute then turned on his heel.

"...Let's go," he said.

The girls rubbed their eyes—several times—and nodded.

Inside the room it was dimly lit. Fairly spacious—the walls and ceiling were lost in shadow. All they could make out was the floor, and the pattern that led farther in, beckoning them.

It was quiet. So quiet, Masato could hear lingering sniffles.

They walked forward, no one speaking. Then someone slapped him hard on the back.

Wise, of course. She hit him a few more times, lashing out—but there was no strength behind the blows.

"I think my tear ducts are broken," she said.

"Yeah, I can tell. I held out, though! I'm a man." He said that last bit in Fratello's voice.

"Um, I don't think now's the time to be such a hard-ass. What use is masculinity anyway?"

"I seem to recall hearing this place has something that will make the Hero of the Heavens cry with joy."

"Yes! That was written on the quest posting! I remember it distinctly!"

That stopped Masato in his tracks.

"Oh, yeah. I totally forgot...but..."

He looked around. No signs of anything.

So they walked some more. Nothing but darkness. No treasures, not even a support pillar.

But at last, they found an exit. A small, doorless gate.

Beyond this gate was a space clearly not of the same world—perhaps some other dimension. Framed by flowers in full bloom, white stairs stretched upward—as if they led to Heaven.

Masato stopped outside the entrance.

"Seriously, nothing here? ...I had such hopes, too."

"Hopes for what, Masato?" Porta asked.

"Perhaps something that would make him cry with joy," said Medhi. "Or flying enemies, or the strongest power or sword in the world."

"Yeah, sounds right. You'd expect those to be hidden in the last dungeon. Any gamer would be salty if you accidentally beat the game without picking that stuff up...," said Wise. "Oh, hang on. Is that why he'll end up crying?"

"Precisely. He's sure there must be something, scours the place top to bottom, yet winds up with only tears for his trouble."

"That'd definitely make me cry, but not for joy! This game isn't that heartless. No, I meant..." He turned back, staring into the void beyond. "It would've been nice if this place had been filled with the memories of all this world's citizens. I mean, their memories of us are sealed away somewhere, right? If we could release them and let everybody remember us again..."

Like Hahako had done for her daughters. Or would that just cause more grief?

Masato shook his head. "No, maybe this is better. Maybe they're better off forgetting us. All we'd be able to do is say good-bye. And that'd make things harder for everyone..."

But before he could say anything else...

"Boooo! Don't go getting all gloomy on me."

He heard a voice—Mone's voice.

A single speck of light appeared in the darkness then burst, and suddenly Mone appeared. She came running toward the party and threw her arms around Masato, nuzzling her cheek against his chest.

"Gotcha! Tee-hee! *Rubrub. Rubrub!* Recharging spoilmeter!"

"M-Mone? Why are you here...?"

"It's not *just* me! Ta-da!"

Countless beads of light appeared at once before bursting, the resulting flash so bright, the party closed their eyes...

And when they opened them, the darkened hall was filled with people.

Everyone from Catharn. From Maman Village. Mr. Burly and his students. Pocchi, Pocchi's mom, the roustabouts, and the members of

Mom's Guild. The casino owner and staff. The beastkin mom Growl-ette and everyone else from the World Matriarchal Arts Tournament. And so many more.

Everyone they'd met, all smiling through tears.

And everyone was calling their names.

Mone finished dampening Masato's shirt with her own tears before gently stepping back.

"I'd love to cuddle more, but I'll spare you. I can't stay attached to you forever, Masato."

"Oh? Then you've grown, too, Mone."

"Heh-heh. You bet! ...Masato, Wise, Medhi, Porta...this is good-bye. But don't worry! I won't forget you. All of us are gonna remember. So you don't need to cry those tears of joy, Masato."

"...I'm *not* crying."

"Heh-heh-heh. Sure, let's say you aren't. You just really look like you are. Anyway, Masato, you said all you could do was say good-bye, but that's not true. We know something else to send you off with. Okay, everybody!"

The crowd spoke as one:

"Thank you for adventuring in our world!"

Masato bowed his head low.

"I should be thanking you. You've all done so much for me! Thank you!"

The girls each bowed in turn. They were sobbing too hard to get many words out, but they said their thank-yous as well.

When Masato looked up again, Mone's face was a mess with tears, but she smiled anyway.

"Okay! Then on you go. Run for it! Don't even think about turning around! Go! Now!"

"You got it!"

The Hero's party turned and raced through the door.

And as they did...

She's here!

He felt his mother coming.

They started running up the white staircase, and edges of the sky began to twist. As effortlessly as passing through curtains, beautifully pale oversized fingers parted space itself, the body following right behind.

It was MegaMamako's smiling face.

"Hee-hee-hee! Ma-kun, I found you! Our game of tag is alllll done."

"You finally made it, huh, Mom?"

"Hurry, Masato! We already said good-bye! If we get caught and dragged back, we'll look super pathetic!"

"For the sake of everyone who saw us off, we must complete our journey here!"

"You have to reach the transport point, Masato! Go on ahead! I'll slow Mama down!"

"Porta... Okay! I'll trust you!"

"Yes! I've got this!" Porta had been lagging behind anyway, and now she stopped dead, turning to face MegaMamako.

"Oh my, Porta! Are you going up against me?"

"That's right! I'm going to use the power of me and Mommy's tight-knit bond to stop you! Here goes!"

Porta took Piita and Piitamama off her shoulder bag and held them high. The dolls were wearing the power-up outfits Dark-Mom Death-mother had made for them, and they grew beyond Pretty Prodigious size into…P-P-P-P-Pretty Prodigious size!

Piita and Piitamama were now about half MegaMamako's size, and each of them grabbed on to one of her legs, not letting go.

"Oh my. Oh dear. My legs won't move at all! You're so strong."

"I did it! Now Mama can't chase after Masato! We win!"

"Hee-hee-hee… I don't know about *that*."

"Huh?"

MegaMamako smiled happily and knelt down. Wings unfurled on her back—one made from trees and leaves and earthy materials, the other from seaweed and other aquatic materials.

"Whoaaaaaa! Mama grew wings!"

"This is MegaMommy's second form! Okay, Porta dear, careful the wind doesn't send you flying! Here I go!"

"Aiiiiieeee!"

A single flap of her wings, and MegaMamako's massive form took to the air. Piita and Piitamama were still clinging to her legs, and she was after Masato again. He, Wise, and Medhi were only halfway up the stairs.

They could just make out the top, but flying MegaMamako was closing in.

"Ma-kun, look at me! Mommy's flying! My wings go flappy flap!"
Flappy flap.

"Yo, stop! The wind pressure's nuts! We'll be blown away! ...Argh, how is my mom so broken?! What's even happening?!"

"Pretty obvious, duh! She's just being the same old OP Mamako! Only one option left... Medhi!"

"Wise and I will slow her down. Masato, run for it!"

"Gotcha! Thanks!"

Masato never broke stride.

Wise and Medhi stopped, facing MegaMamako.

"Okay, Mamako. I know you're in a hurry, but you've gotta go through us first."

"Oh, I don't mind. It sounds like I need to give you both another mom interview."

"You mean you want to check if we're suitable to be Masato's life partner, then?"

"Hee-hee. More or less!"

"Augh! Th-that was just stuff our moms made up...but sure, it works in our favor here. Not like there's *no* chance of that happening!"

"Then let's get started. What would the two of you do for your future husband?"

"An easy question," said Medhi. "If his mother starts acting too selfish..."

"Then it's the wife's job to show her who's boss!" Wise had her tome in hand and was pouring all her magic power into it.

Unable to withstand the sheer quantity of magic, the tome split apart, and the pages flew in all directions, forming a massive magic circle around her.

"The ultimate magic my mom taught me—it takes everything I've got. Prepare yourself for a one-time-only super-ultimate spell!"

"G-gosh, Wise! You're even sacrificing your bust size—your very life is on the line! ...I shouldn't point that out, though."

"You just did! And I'm not sacrificing squat, Medhi!"

"It was a joke. I wasn't being mean. Promise!"

"Fine, whatever. That's just how you communicate, Medhi. I know you act all evil, but you're actually nice deep down. If you were truly that nasty, we'd never have gotten along so well."

"Heh-heh-heh. I'm so glad you understand me." Medhi smiled happily, but quickly turned grim, focusing her attention on her staff. "Then I shall unleash the power my mother granted me... Conforto Staff, now is the time to unleash my true self!"

Dark power erupted from her every pore—and that, too, was instantly blown away by a pure white light that shone from Medhi's very core.

And as the light faded, Medhi became a dragon. Pure white scales, not a trace of corruption. Angelic wings. And where her visage had once been terrifying, now she was almost divine.

Medhi transformed into Holy Medhidragon!

"WISE, I'M READY WHEN YOU ARE."

"Roger that. All right, Mamako! Here goes nothing!"

"Yes, go right ahead. Let's see how you 'show me who's boss'!"

MegaMamako reached out her hands, trying to sweep Wise and Holy Medhidragon into a MegaMom embrace. If they got caught in that, they'd be relentlessly cuddled. And given MegaMamako's size, fleeing was not an option. They had to stop those arms from reaching Masato—to protect his wishes.

Wise and Medhi attacked.

"Full power! ...*Spara la magia per mirare... Laurea della Madre!*"

This was a wife's nuke of stubbornness, spelling the end of a mother's role.

"I'LL STAKE EVERYTHING ON THIS ATTACK! NEWLYWED BREATH!"

A wife's beam of stubbornness, rocking the foundations of a mother's domain.

Wise's spell hit the oceanic wing while Holy Medhidragon's breath hit the earthen one. Two attacks slammed home, attacking the very nature of motherhood.

A powerful explosion blew the oceanic wing clean off! A gaping hole opened in the earthen wing, and it crumbled apart!

No longer capable of flight, MegaMamako crashed to the ground at the edge of the stairs.

"Goodness! Oh dear! You certainly showed me... My, myyy...!"

"Yes, we did it! ...But that's...all I've got left..."

"SAME HERE... THAT WAS MY LIMIT..."

Wise slumped to the ground. Holy Medhidragon collapsed onto the stairs, changing back to her original form. Neither could get up again.

But that was also true for MegaMamako. P-P-P-Pretty Prodigious Piita and Piitamamako had her legs held tight, clinging to her knees. She couldn't fly, let alone move at all—they had MegaMamako perfectly restrained.

"...W-we did it!"

"Somehow, yes."

The smiles of a job well done.

Wise and Medhi reached for a high five...

"Hee-hee. Well, I'm glad you both told me exactly how you feel. I'd better catch up with Ma-kun and tell him all about it!"

And just as those words left her mouth, a sphere of mingled crimson and blue shot out of MegaMamako, rocketing between Wise and Medhi.

Bound for, of course...

Masato had just climbed the final stair.

"So this is the finish line...?"

He was in a room, neither large nor small, filled with flowers—as if celebrating his victory. And at the center of that was a transport device.

If he stepped onto that, the game was over.

But…

"…I knew she'd come."

Feeling a certain someone approaching, Masato knew he'd need to be armed and ready.

He glanced around—"Oh, good"—and gathered some up, hiding them behind his back.

Just in time, too—she was here.

The mom-colored sphere descended before the transport point. The sphere itself dissolved, and the person within stepped out.

"Hee-hee-hee. Ma-kun, it's Mommy! I'm here!"

Mamako.

She was back to her original height—but her outfit had merged with the earth and the ocean, making her look extra spectacular.

No swords at her hips—instead, there was a crimson ribbon on her right wrist and a deep blue ribbon on her left.

His weapon hidden behind him, Masato moved to face her.

"Seems like you've powered up."

"I have! This is MegaMommy's final form. These ribbons were once the holy two-hit multi-target attack swords!"

"What do they do?"

"Mommy's hugs are now doubled-up full-body embraces. It's a big buff!"

"That is the wrong way to buff yourself, but very you."

"Well, Ma-kun? Ready to leap into Mommy's arms?"

She spread her arms wide. The ribbons on her wrists stretched out— long enough to wrap around every inch of him. Mamako was trying to bind Masato to her.

But before she could…

"The first attack is mine! Mom, brace yourself."

He thrust his hidden weapon toward her.

A carnation bouquet.

"Mom, hear me out."

This surprise attack succeeded, and Mamako's eyes opened wide.

To mother, from son.

"You're scared to go back to the real world, Mom. Right now, we can talk like this—but you're worried if we go home, things'll get awkward between us again. That's why you don't want to stop playing, right?"

Mamako seemed unsure how to respond, but after a moment, she managed a small nod. "...It's not that I don't trust you, Ma-kun. I just can't help fretting."

"That bad, huh?"

"Yes. Children don't stop growing up and changing. You certainly haven't. I barely recognize you. You're being so nice to me now, but... that might change again. I know I shouldn't assume the worst, but..."

"Sheesh, Mom. You're such a worrywart."

"I know! I wish I wasn't. But no matter how old children get, mommies always worry. And your mommy's so frustrated!"

"Don't do the sulky face."

Mamako had puffed out her cheeks, so he shook the bouquet in front of her like he was banishing the bad energy.

Then he got serious.

"I know it's a cliché, but...nobody knows what the future holds. Maybe you're right, and back home, it won't all be fun times. But I might change for the worse even if we do keep playing this game together. Nothing's set in stone. Right?"

"Well...I know, but..."

"So there's no use thinking about it now. What's the point? ...You see, there's actually a much bigger problem going on. One my life may well depend upon."

"Your life?! Wh-what could that be?!" Mamako turned pale.

Masato's expression grew very grave.

"I'm starving. I wanna go home and have something to eat— something you cooked, Mom."

Then he broke into the broadest smile he could muster.

Mamako blinked at him.

"Your son's on the brink of starvation! C'mon, Mom—what are you gonna do?" he asked.

"What else? I mean...there's nothing else I *can* do. I have to rush right home and get cooking, of course! Hrmph."

She shot Masato a pouty look then burst out laughing. Slapping his arm, doubled over with laughter…and a few tears.

So silly. So incredibly silly.

But that was how families talked. A normal, happy, close-knit family.

And that warmed a mom's heart more than any drama, or any adventure.

Mamako took the carnations and linked arms with Masato. "Okay, Ma-kun. What do you want to eat?"

"Eh…anything's fine."

"Oh dear! That answer always worries me."

Families talk like this in any world, in any home.

"Well, we've got requests! I want the usual."

"I'll take whatever you recommend, Mamako."

"Mama, I want the best thing you can make!"

Their party came running up to join them, flinging their arms around Mamako.

"Wow, so many hungry kids," said Masato.

"Hee-hee-hee. You're right! Well, why don't we invite you girls and your mothers over and have one big happy dinner?"

The Hero's party stepped onto the transport device, which wrapped them in a light as warm as a mother's love, and off they went.

Parent and Child Awareness Survey

MMMMMORPG Sequel Prep Vol. 5

Are you close to your child?

We couldn't be closer.

Do you talk with your child? How often?

Every day, from morning to night. So much talking!

Has your child said anything lately that made you happy?

He said he wanted to eat my home cooking. As a mom, that's my favorite thing to hear.

Has your child said anything lately that made you unhappy?

I can't remember a single thing. Hee-hee-hee.

Have you ever gone anywhere with your child?

All across the game world.

Have you learned what your child likes?

The person he loves most is Mommy, and the thing he loves most is my cooking.

Have you learned what your child hates?

I don't think he hates much, but...maybe enemies that don't fly?

What are your child's strong points?

Everything, of course.

What are your child's weak points?

I do wish he'd let me dote on him more...but that might be asking too much.

How was your adventure with your child?

I can truly say we had the time of our lives.

If you have any other opinions or requests, please write them here. These will assist with future service updates.

It was such a lovely game, but it was a real shame that the mommies weren't able to properly thank everyone who helped us. And now that the official launch is here, we can't go back and play some more, right? ...Do you think you can find some way for us to meet again? I sure hope so.

Answers: Mamako Oosuki

Epilogue

A month had passed since Masato beat the game and returned to the real world.

The school day was almost over, and the classroom was abuzz.

"Quiet, everyone. I'm passing this survey around. The last one was a more targeted deal, but this time it's nationwide. Same contents, but it's important, so make sure you fill it out right."

The teacher was handing out a parent-child awareness survey conducted by the Cabinet Office's Department of Policy on Cohesive Society to determine the state of today's youth.

All the booklets were placed at the front row of students and passed to the back. The boy seated in front of Masato turned and handed one over with a flashy smile. "Masato, this is that thing, right?"

"…Thing?"

"You know! The *MMMMMORPG* (official) launch! Fill this thing out right, and you get to play!"

"I dunno anything about that."

"Psh, quit lying. You were out of school for ages doing some secret government program. That was the beta, right? *Everyone* knows. C'mon, spill the beans. What do I put here?"

"Hey! No talking! Answer the survey. Or do I have to confiscate your form?"

"Crap, not that!" The boy hastily faced front.

The room got very quiet. Everyone was focused. No one objected when the class ran overtime. The students were taking this way more seriously than any school exam.

Only one student was just writing down whatever.

I'm sure this is helping them pick users, but...

Masato could no longer take part. That was a bit sad, but he knew why. And so he just put the most honest answers he could.

He paused, staring out the window. It was a sunny day here in the real world. Blue skies.

Then something moved at the corner of his eye: a small figure with a red backpack, over by the gates.

Masato's princess, waiting for him. He'd better wrap this survey up.

Last question:

If you went on an adventure with your mom, would you become closer?

Masato's answer?

"Duh. I know I did."

He shook his head, then shouldered his backpack and stood up.

As he left the gate, his sixth-grade princess started waving.

"Masatooo! I'm over here!"

"Hey! Sorry I'm running late, Porta—I mean, Moko."

"Bwuh...?!"

She seemed surprised to hear her real name.

"Wh-what? Isn't that your name? I didn't get it wrong, did I?"

"N-no! You're right. That's my name, but...um, it just feels weird!"

Those cheeks of hers looked a bit red. Porta—aka Moko—covered them with her hands, frowning. Even she seemed unsure why Masato using her real name had made her jump.

"Um, um...t-today's a game friends gathering, so let's stick with Porta," she said.

"Okay. Good point, Porta. We've gotta collect Wise and Medhi, and then our party's ready for adventure."

"Yes!"

The two of them walked off together, headed for the train station.

As they chatted about good game times, Masato's pocket vibrated—an incoming call. When he looked, it was from his father, Hayato.

"Porta, sorry, lemme take this... Hello?"

"Hi, Masato. It's your dad! Is now a good time? I'm afraid I've got some bad news..."

"You can't join us for dinner?"

"That's right. Thanks for the invite, though."

"No, I get it. You've got work to do. But is that other person—?"

"Hotta's still coming. Admin meetings wrapped up in the AM. I can infooorm you she went running pell-mell out the meeting room screeching Moko's name."

Good infooormation. "Porta, your mom's coming." "Yay! I'm so happy!" She was literally jumping for joy. Adorbs.

"Oh, right. Speaking of infooormation..."

"Mm? What?"

"Shirase isn't taking time off; she'll be on the clock. In other words, she's coming to dinner in an official capacity. I don't know the details, but... Ugh, I've gotta go. Talk to you later!"

"Uh, hang in there..."

Hayato hung up. Masato scratched his head, and Porta blinked up at him, wondering what was going on. Super adorable.

They started walking again. Time sure flew by when they talked. They reached the station in a heartbeat.

The Oosuki home was a short walk from the other side of the shopping district. But first, they stopped outside a small supermarket in the area.

"This is where Wise is working, right?"

"Yes! Mom Superstore!"

"Mom's favorite shop, and apparently Wise got the job because Mom recommended her... I had no idea she lived only three stops away. Still, why work all the way out *here*?"

"Because it's close to her house!"

"It really isn't, though."

It was close to *someone's* house, just not Wise's.

Inside the grocery store, they headed to the veggie stands—and soon found who they were looking for.

"So you've been working all day? That sounds exhausting..."

"Yeah, school's closed 'cause today's the anniversary of its founding. If I've got the time, I gotta earn some dough. That's how we poor folks live."

"Fascinating. And here I took a taxi from the station, a distance I could easily have walked."

"Don't rub it in, heiress."

Stacking napa cabbage was a girl with pigtails shaped like chocolate cornets and a grocery apron over her school's skirt-and-blouse uniform. Next to her, looking rather bored, was a beautiful girl in a sailor uniform.

The rest of Masato's party.

"Yo, Wise, or Genya, or is it Wise? ...And uh..."

"Oh, hello, Masato. I'm perfectly fine with Medhi." *Smile.*

The smiling sailor-style stunner was Medhi.

However...

"Gawd, Masato. You know her real name. It's *Elise*. So fancy, so classy! Perfect für you, Elise. *Snort.*"

"What was that just now, Genya? Do you have a problem with my name? Funny, my fists seem to have your name written all over them. Could you check and see if it's written on my foot, too?" ... *Rummmble...*

"Eep! I can see her dark power even in the real world!"

A girl named for a famous piano composition and the girl with a host's stage name stared each other down, but before the cat fight could engage in earnest—"Nope, stop!" Masato stepped in. "We're all game friends here, so let's stick with our game names! Okay?"

"Yes, that seems the best course of action. Wise, we have an errand to run. Good luck with your work."

"Hey, don't try and leave me here! I just gotta punch out, so wait up a second."

"Yes! All four of us should go to Masato's house together!"

The conversation wandered as they walked. This road had no monsters or encounters. It was just the four of them.

"...Hey, guys...say we could go back to the game world... You know, hypothetically...," Masato began.

"I think I'd go for a Warrior job this time. I wanna give physical attacks a try," Wise replied. "Medhi's enough magic for us all."

"No, I was thinking I'd like to be a Warrior myself. Perhaps a Knight," said Medhi. "Then Porta can be our Mage."

"Okay! I'd love to use magic!"

"But Masato's the Normal Hero."

"The normal leader."

"I'm good with Hero, but do we have to stick with Normal? And..."

Their partying up again seemed to be a given. None of the girls seemed to have any doubts about that, and Masato couldn't help smiling. But that smile soon grew a little forlorn.

"I guess that's not in the cards, though."

"Yeah...the official version launched, but we're not part of it."

"Unless something *very* unexpected happens, we can assume it'll stay that way."

"I hope something very unexpected does happen!"

"Yep. For now, we can only hope... But tonight we've got our usual Hero's party together for a parent-child dinner with everyone's moms in tow. It's gonna be awesome!"

""""Woo!"""""

A cheer echoed through the quiet streets—and soon the group reached the Oosuki home.

Once inside, they found four sets of women's shoes, all in a row. The moms were already here...but the house was oddly silent.

They headed for the living room. Masato opened the door, but everything looked normal—no party prep at all.

"Hello," Shirase said, sipping a cup of tea. "I can inform you that I have arrived—as my name is Shirase."

She was alone.

"Just you, Shirase? No moms?"

"I've had them step away. Now, to business! If I may have your attention for a moment. Let me begin with the necessary introductions. My ID." Shirase stood up, came over to them, and held up the ID card hanging from her neck.

"Cabinet Office, Department of Policy on Cohesive Society, External Surveyor Masumi Shirase. Yeah, we know," said Wise.

"Why the formality?" Medhi asked Shirase.

"I'm simply following proper protocol for conveying a request from the government. As the test players who cleared the *MMMMMORPG* (working title) beta, we'd appreciate your assistance developing the sequel."

"Sequel?" said Masato. "By sequel, you mean… No way!"

"The core system, your adventure records, characters, and memories are all carried over. And it remains a full-dive online game powered by mystery technology. This time you'll be focusing on quests concerning the darker aspects of society."

"And by help, you mean…? I can't believe it! C-c-can we?" said Porta.

"Heh-heh-heh. That's right! Look over there."

Shirase pointed at the TV screen. She'd brought Masato's computer tower downstairs and hooked it up, using the TV as a monitor.

The party ran over to the screen.

"Seriously?! Is this real?! No joke?!"

"Is everybody ready? Here we go—a very unexpected happening from me, Shirase!"

"Talk about unexpected!"

Shirase picked up the remote, pressed a button…and the screen lit up!

"We mommies are off on an adventure! Woo!"

""""Woo!""""

Mamako, Kazuno, Medhimama, and Dark-Mom Deathmother appeared on-screen, all four mothers raising their firsts and heading out into the distance.

"I can inform you that this unbelievably unexpected all-mom adventure has now begun."

"Back uuuuuuuuuup! Mom?! *Everyone's* moms?! You're just ditching us kids?!"

As Masato glared at the screen, Mamako looked up.

"Oh? I feel Ma-kun looking at me! Which way? Over here? That's right! Ma-kun, it's Mommy!" *Wave.*

"Why is she waving?! And how did she know?!"

> "Your mommies are off on a little adventure. We'll be back by dinner, don't worry. If you want to adventure with me, Ma-kun, then it's your turn to chase after me! I don't mind. Can you all catch up to your mommies? It won't be easy! Hee-hee."

"You heard her! First quest: Get into the game world and catch our moms!"

""""Woo!"""""

Light flooded out of the screen, and their hearts pounded with excitement. Shirase almost "accidentally" pressed the power switch, but thought better of it.

A new journey!

"Mom, I'm coming! We're mom-along adventurers through and through!"

Once a family always a family. The adventure never ends.

And theirs was just beginning.

THE END

Afterword

Thank you, everyone. This is Inaka.

Journeying through a game world—with your mom?! A whole new kind of momcom adventure! That was the pitch for this series—and this was how it ended.

I can't thank my readers enough.

Before debuting with this title, I did my time in the submission trenches. I have many characters that never saw the light of day. They were born—and went nowhere.

Pour one out for them.

Thanks to everyone's support, I was able to write this series to its natural conclusion.

Characters, characters, my kingdom for characters. Lo, do they vanish into that sweet night, raging against their creator's whim. The characters in this series bore the burden of all those who came before, and writing them brought me endless joy.

I am so grateful.

Thank you.

I can't say it enough.

To everyone involved:

My editor, the editorial department, publishers, designers, proofreaders, printers, binders, sales reps, and booksellers.

Meicha, who drew the manga, and the manga editors.

Everyone who helped with the audiobooks.

Everyone involved with the anime—the producers, director, staff, and cast.

And to Iida Pochi.

Thank you—each and every one of you. Well done.

I'll never forget what you did for me.

I pray you will all produce more work, in health and happiness.

And if we have the opportunity to work together again, I would be honored.

Finally...

I'd hoped to have a family anecdote, but I haven't been home yet.

My sister's family is having a dinner to celebrate both my father's successful animism (aneurysm?) clipping surgery and his dumb son's series conclusion.

It's been a while since we've all been together.

My mother says she wants the expensive muscats, the ones we usually don't buy.

Don't worry, I'll buy 'em for you.

So...

While I wait for that dinner date, I'll work on the plot for my next book.

I hope we meet again.

Spring 2020, Dachima Inaka